HELL'S ACRES

When gambler Smoke Cavendish is attacked and robbed of his poker winnings, his assailants leave him to die in the desert. Determined to survive, he stumbles into Hell's Acres, a town of desolation, where the townsfolk are under the boot of Mark Tarlton and his ruthless gunhawks. There, Smoke meets the beautiful Trixie Lee, but soon he clashes with Tarlton, and finds himself gambling for the highest stakes — his life, and the life of the woman he loves.

Books by John Russell Fearn
in the Linford Western Library:

NAVAJO VENGEANCE
MERRIDEW FOLLOWS THE TRAIL
THUNDER VALLEY

JOHN RUSSELL FEARN

HELL'S ACRES

Complete and Unabridged

LINFORD
Leicester

First published in Great Britain in 2000
Originally published in paperback as
Hell's Acres by Mick McCoy

First Linford Edition
published 2007

All characters and incidents in this book are
fictitious. Any resemblance to a living person,
or to an actual occurrence, is accidental.

British Library CIP Data

Fearn, John Russell, *1908 – 1960*
    Hell's Acres.—Large print ed.—
    Linford western library
    1. Western stories
    2. Large type books
    I. Title II. McCoy, Mick, *1908 – 1960*
    823.9'12 [F]

    ISBN 978–1–84617–965–5

Published by
F. A. Thorpe (Publishing)
Anstey, Leicestershire

Set by Words & Graphics Ltd.
Anstey, Leicestershire
Printed and bound in Great Britain by
T. J. International Ltd., Padstow, Cornwall

This book is printed on acid-free paper

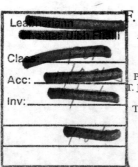

1

Nothing but the dust, the warm wind, and the blaze of the sun. Never a cloud across his blinding face. Sparse high cirrus cloud streaked casually across the cobalt dome to the south — and on the scorching sandy trail below, its monotony broken only by giant Saguaro cactus here and there, a man rode steadily.

He was young, leathery, and bestrode his sorrel with an air of resolution. He was a man hardened to these blistering wastes, a man with the red dust grimed into his skin, a man whose eyes were as blue as the sky itself.

He was two days out from Dodge City in Kansas, heading northwards, in the direction of Smoky Hill Fork. This was not his destination. He planned to ride straight out of Kansas and into Nebraska. There was a man out there at the Yellow-V spread, who had offered him a job as foreman. Not that he wanted it, only he had to keep on living. It was not easy to do so either when cursed with the soul of a gambler. Larry 'Smoke' Cavendish had it both ways. His father and mother had both been gamblers, and had lost. Smoke had it in his blood and was having a mighty tough time getting rid of it. He had cleaned up a thousand greenbacks in Dodge City and then hit leather for the north. And here he was, his tired horse loping on steadily in the afternoon glare.

It was around four when he came to a water-hole. He stopped, watered his horse, drank his own fill, and then settled down to rest for a while. The trident-shaped cacti did not afford much cover from the glare, but it was better than nothing. For a while the horse slept, head nodding, sweat gleaming on his silken sides.

Then, on again. By the time the evening was setting in Smoke had left the desert region behind and was following a lonely, little used path through the foothills of a low mountain range. It was cooler here, and he drank in the wine-like air gratefully. The horse, too, moved with more energy.

'I reckon we'll find somewheres around here to stop for the night, Pal,' Smoke said, looking about him. 'Bit further on mebbe there'll be an outcropping.'

He broke off, looking about him sharply. Abruptly there had come the crack of a rifle. A slug whined dangerously close and rock chippings flew out of the cliff face at Smoke's side. His eyes glinting, he whipped out his right hand Colt, and fired twice in the direction whence the shot had come — apparently from a point about twenty feet up on his right.

Hardly had the echo of his shots died away before another bullet whanged. This time it found its mark and the horse whinneyed. Its forelegs buckled and Smoke found himself pitching over the wounded animal's head. He hit the dust and rolled several feet.

Yanking out his twin gun he looked about him — but nothing happened. Then he switched his attention to the horse. It was writhing helplessly, trying to get up and failing. It was one of those moments which no Westerner can ever forget. He had to shoot a faithful friend — and did. His powerful face sweating, he stood with cordite fumes curling round his nostrils and watched the animal relax into quivering death.

Then he swung, staring up at the rimrock.

'Come outa there, you dirty side-winders!' he yelled. 'That is if you ain't plain scared!'

'Who's scared?' a voice asked drily.

Smoke twisted round and beheld three gunmen to the back of him. All had bandanna kerchiefs up to their eyes. One of them was wearing a white Stetson rusted to yellow with age. All three men held their guns rock steady. Smoke muttered to himself, realizing that whilst he had been disposing of his horse the men had come from their perch and gathered behind him.

'Best drop yuh hardware, fella,' advised Yellow Hat.

Smoke knew better than to argue. His pearl-handled Colts dropped into the dust from his upraised hands. One of the men came forward and picked them up, then he shoved them in his belt.

'What's the idea?' Smoke asked bitterly. 'I'm no big shot who's worth rubbing out. I'm little more than a saddle tramp on my way through.'

'A saddle tramp with a thousand dollars who's too free with his tongue,' Yellow Hat said drily. 'Yuh shouldn't go shootin' off yuh mouth about it if yuh don't want to lose yuh winnings.'

Smoke frowned. 'What the hell are you talking about?'

'Yuh've bin followed from Dodge City, fella,' Yellow Hat explained. 'We wus in the saloon of the Last Frontier when yuh made yuh thousand dollars at the gaming table. Yuh got too much likker inside uv yuh an' talked about it. An' yuh also sed yuh was headin' north fur Nebraska. Simple enough ter keep track uv yuh, even if we did go a long way round ter keep frum bein' seen. I'll trouble yuh fur that thousand bucks.'

'You dirty, no-account parasites!' Smoke yelled at them. 'Nothing better t'do than tail a guy whose made some money the hard way — an' that's what gambling is, believe me! Shot my horse from under me and now — '

Yellow Hat jerked his head. 'Save the spiel, fella. Hand over that money. Jed, fix it up.'

The man who had taken the guns obeyed. He came forward and began to pat Smoke's pockets. When he arrived at a bulging shirt pocket he grinned — but only for a moment. Suddenly regardless of guns and everything else Smoke smashed out his right fist with all the power of his steel-muscled arm. Jed took the impact straight on the chin and crashed into the dust, blood oozing between his clenched teeth.

A gun exploded. Smoke felt hell tear into his shoulder and there was a warm trickle down his arm. He dived and brought Yellow Hat crashing. But that was as far as he got. A gun butt slammed at the back of his ear and he sprawled, his senses swimming but not deserting him entirely. Dazed, he saw Yellow Hat get up and take the money which Jed handed to him. Then the remaining man picked up a rifle which was propped against the racks. Putting it to his shoulder he aimed it straight at Smoke.

'Put that dad-blamed thing down,' Yellow Hat snapped. 'We ain't killers — not yet. The rap's too tough. Just frisking a guy is enough. Now let's beat it.'

They turned and as he staggered to his feet, holding his damaged shoulder, Smoke watched their retreating backs. In a moment or two the rocks had hidden them. Before long he heard the sound of hoofbeats echoing from the mountain face and slowly diminishing with distance.

Smoke looked about him, his face grim. His horse was dead, his money had gone, and they'd parked hot lead in his shoulder. The anguish of it was getting worse. Without some medical attention anything might happen.

Gritting his teeth, he gave one final glance at his horse and then staggered his way along the dusty, narrow trail. He kept on going, with rests, until he had reached a point where he could gain a better view of his surroundings. Looking over a rocky ledge he saw that the cut through the foothills ended about here and led down into a twilit valley. There was still enough light for him to descry a town of sorts — ramshackle like all of them in this tough, lawless region, but at least a sanctuary where he might get a rest, a drink, and a sawbones.

It was sheer will-power and iron physique which kept him going, though he had to rest several times on the way.

By the time he had descended the valley side the abrupt transition from day to night was complete, and kerosene lamps were casting their uncertain glimmer on the town's main street.

Some of the jumble of buildings had lights in them. The brightest glare of all came from a particularly gaudy-faced saloon. On the signboard outside the batwings and across the half-concealed windows were the words — Hell's Acres. Beyond the fact that it seemed to him a curious name for a drinking and gaming hall, Smoke gave it no more thought. In fact, at the moment, his only idea was to get inside and try and fix himself up.

Unsteadily, still holding his blood-soddened shoulder, he lurched through the batwings and looked around him. At this hour of the evening there were not many customers in the place, and those who were present surveyed him in surprise. Their eyes followed him as he moved unsteadily towards the bar.

'Looks like yore in a bad way, stranger,' the bald-headed barkeep commented. 'Yuh want that shoulder fixin'.'

'You don't have t'tell me,' Smoke panted. 'Give me a brandy — quick. I got the notion I might pass out.'

The brandy was handed to him and he swallowed it quickly — then his notion came true and he did pass out. The next thing he realized was that he was on his back on a horsehair sofa with a rolled-up coat for a pillow. He had been stripped to the waist and wadding was bound in place on his injured shoulder. He moved slightly and looked about him. He saw three faces, and beyond them the outline of an office. There was a calendar on the wall, two gun belts, filing cabinets, pictures of women in frills doing the can-can . . .

'Thanks,' Smoke muttered gratefully. 'I reckon my shoulder feels a whole heap better.'

'You'll be okay,' one of the faces said,

his voice matter of fact. 'I'm Doc Jones. I'm on hand if you need me — further down the street. I got the slug out and you're healthy enough to do the rest yourself, I guess.' ·

With that he turned away and a moment afterwards the door closed. Smoke was left to study the remaining two faces. One was that of a fortyish, good-looking man with a straight nose, dark eyes, and finely moulded chin. His mouth was very firm, even cruel, and it seemed hard work for him to smile. For the rest of him there was a white shield of shirt front and a shoestring tie, black hair gleaming in the oil-light, fancy flowered waistcoat and a black jacket with silk revers.

'I'm Mark Tarlton,' he said briefly. 'I own Hell's Acres.'

'This saloon, you mean?' Smoke asked.

'More than that — the town. The whole town is called Hell's Acres, but my place was here before it grew.'

Smoke moved his eyes to the second

face. It belonged to a girl of perhaps twenty-three or five. She was wearing a sequinned gown cut low to her breasts and exposing the alabaster white of rounded shoulders and arms. A jewelled locket was glinting about her throat. She was very blonde, and even without the make-up would have been unusually good-looking — though just now there was a sullen petulance about her full mouth.

'You a nurse?' Smoke grinned. 'If so I sure hope I'm going to be a long time recovering.'

'She's Trixie Lee,' Tarlton answered, before she could speak. 'My hostess, singer, and giver-all. She figgered she might be able to help, so I let her — regarding you, I mean.'

'Like taking my shirt off?' Smoke suggested.

'Just that,' Trixie said, and the sullen look vanished as she smiled. It was a bright, engaging smile which showed uneven but very white teeth.

Smoke made an effort to rise, but he

did not succeed very well — until the soft, warm arm of Trixie behind his shoulders helped him. So, gradually, he achieved a sitting position and rubbed his face slowly.

'I owe you folks plenty,' he said. 'Come to think of it I owe for a brandy, too.'

'On the house.' Tarlton's voice was cryptic. 'As for any other money you may owe — forget it. You haven't any, anyway, if your shirt pockets are a guide.'

'Forgotten my pants?' Smoke asked drily.

Tarlton gave him a level stare. 'No. I didn't find any there, either.'

There was a momentary silence, then with Trixie's help Smoke got slowly to his feet. He was less groggy than he had expected, but he liked the girl's arm across his back and so did not make an immediate recovery.

'Time I looked more like a gentleman,' he said, nodding to his ripped shirt nearby. 'If I ever can in that thing.

Looks like the doc ripped the sleeve out.'

'You can have a shirt of mine,' Tarlton said. 'We're about the same build. Go get one out of my private room, Trixie.'

She shook her blonde head. 'Not me, Mark. If anything else went from your office at the same time you'd only have me to blame. I'm not taking that kind of a risk.'

Smoke glanced from one to the other. 'What gives? Don't you trust a lady, Tarlton?'

'Sure I do — an' she knows it. She's just kidding.'

Tarlton gave a sour smile which merged into an angry glance, then he turned and left the office. Smoke looked at the girl and found her big grey eyes fixed upon him.

'Tarlton has a private room as well as an office, then?' Smoke asked.

'Yes. Sort of room where he — he can't be disturbed. Useful sometimes, like when he and me are together.'

Trixie hesitated, then removed her arm from behind Smoke's broad back. 'Don't get me wrong, mister. I'm not the kind of girl you may be thinking.'

Smoke shrugged. 'Would that matter to me? I'm only passing through.'

She surveyed him for a moment. 'You've got mighty big muscles, stranger — big as Mark's. Only you're different. I guess you're sort of friendly, and that's more than he is. It makes an awful difference to a girl sometimes if a man will smile at her the right way.'

'You mean you're turned loose amongst the wolves?' Smoke asked.

'You might call it that. He runs everything, including me. It's nice to find a man who's — different.'

Smoke was trying to puzzle this one out when Mark Tarlton returned with a shirt over his arm. He handed it across and watched in tight-lipped silence whilst Trixie gave Smoke a hand to get the sleeve over his damaged shoulder and arm. In the end the job was done — or almost. She tore a piece from the hem of her voluminous skirt and formed it into a rough sling. When she finished Smoke was entirely comfortable, and Tarlton was cynically watchful.

'How'd you get into this mess, stranger?' he asked.

'Three owl-hooters shot me up.' Smoke turned to him. 'Took a thousand dollars I won gambling at Dodge City. Trailed me, so they said. Shot my horse from under me, too. I guess I've nothing left but the clothes I've got on — and even the shirt's borrowed.'

'Heading any place in particular?' Tarlton enquired.

'I was making for Nebraska. I've a foreman's job there — even though I don't want it. How I finish the trip I don't know. I sure can't afford a horse.'

Tarlton was silent, considering. After a moment or two he asked another question.

'So you're a gambler? Good! I like a man who ain't afraid to take a chance. How's about trying your luck on my wheel?'

'With what?'

'It might be arranged.'

Smoke shook his head. 'No dice, Tarlton, thanks all the same. If I lost I'd be unable to pay, and that isn't my way. Just give me another drink on the house, then I'll be on my way. I reckon I can figger out my own problems . . . '

'I'm not that hard-hearted,' Tarlton said drily. 'Better rest up here for tonight and get your shoulder better. I'll see you get a meal. Tomorrow mebbe we can talk. I can even use a man, if you're willing.'

'Doing what?'

'I dunno yet; have ta think about it. Anyways, I must get back into the saloon. Trixie will fix you some food — and make it quick, Trixie. You're on in ten minutes.'

With that Tarlton left, but not before he had given the girl a meaningful glance which escaped Smoke's notice. She turned to him again and forced him to sit down on the sofa once more. Quietly she settled beside him.

'What is your name, stranger?' she murmured.

'Smoke Cavendish. I've another name but I prefer 'Smoke'.'

'You're not telling the truth when you say you've nothing of value except your clothes,' she continued. 'What about those two small gold nuggets sewn into the cuff of your pants?'

Smoke's expression changed. 'How do you know about 'em?'

'Mark found them — or at least he found something hard when he lifted you on to this sofa. He cut the stitching far enough to see gold, then had me sew the cuff back again. He's that kind of man; nothing escapes him.'

'So?' Smoke watched the girl's delicate features intently.

'So you're not penniless. At rough guess, according to Mark, those nuggets are worth around five hundred dollars. Why not use them for a gamble and — '

'No.' Smoke got to his feet again and shook his head. 'I guess I've always had those two nuggets ever since my old man died. He always carried 'em for luck, and I'm doing the same.'

'Call it luck to be without money and five hundred in nuggets sewn in your britches?'

Smoke hesitated. Then the girl had risen and came over to him. In spite of his backward movement one of her soft arms coiled gently round the back of his neck. He had liked her lips from the moment he had first scen her; they were full, moist, and at the moment only an inch from his own. An elusive perfume was rising from her hair.

'Don't be foolish,' she whispered. 'Turn your five hundred into five thousand, then you can do as you like. I'll be your good luck charm.'

'My what?' Smoke tried to gently push her away with his free arm, but she was not to be moved.

'Your mascot, if you wish. I like you well enough to be just that. I don't see how you can miss.'

Smoke hesitated, looking into her

grey eyes and at that provocative mouth. Then with a grin he made a real effort to push her away, and succeeded. She took it passively, but she gave a sigh just the same.

'All right, Smoke, if you want to be tough about it. Go out with your nuggets in your pants, tramp your feet to death, die of thirst — do what any sucker out here does. Rot! I thought you were an intelligent man, but mebbe you're just like all the rest.'

She swung on her heel, pausing when she reached the door. Her cleanly cut features werc contemptuous.

'I'll have a meal fixed for you; after that go when you feel like it.'

She half-opened the door, but before she could pass beyond it Smoke had moved forward. He caught her upper arm and held it tightly. She waited, her grey eyes fixed on his rough-hewn features. Then almost before she realized it he had kissed her — solidly.

'That's all the thanks I can give right now and you seemed to be asking for it,' he grinned. 'But don't get the idea I do it regular, Trixie. Women don't count much to me. I guess they never do to a gambler.'

'You're no gambler,' she said seriously. 'You won't even take a chance with two nuggets.'

'That's where you're wrong.' He released her arm and gave a gentle pat under her rounded chin. 'I guess there's a lot of truth in what you've been saying. I'm cornered, and some money from somewheres is the only answer . . . Get me that meal and another drink, then I'm going into that hall and turn these nuggets into mountains.'

Trixie's grey eyes brightened. She gave a quick nod and then left the office. Smoke wagged his head admiringly to himself and wandered back to the centre of the room. He surveyed the various standbys for a moment, decided there was nothing interesting, and finally took a cigarette from the bark-coloured box on the desk. By the time he had quarter consumed it Trixie was back with beef sandwiches and a glass full of foaming beer.

She did not eat or drink herself. Sitting at the opposite side of the desk she seemed content to watch Smoke pack away the meal. In between mouthfuls he asked questions.

'A good-sized city looks more like your mark than a dump like this, Trixie. How come?'

'I moved in with Mark,' she explained.

'Like that, huh? You mean you're engaged to him?'

'To that lug?' She threw back her blonde head and laughed. 'Not I! Not because he hasn't asked me but because I don't like him. Anything in skirts is his hobby, only I'm kind of particular . . . I want a clean, open-air man if I can find one. Like you, for instance.'

'Selling yourself just like that, eh?' Smoke grinned and swallowed more beer. 'Like I told you, lady, women don't count much to me.'

'I'm not in the general run, Smoke. I've got looks — and I know it. I've got a figure and I know that too. I sell them both to Mark for a few bucks a week. I started off in Denver — that was where I met Mark — and I've been with him ever since.'

'Yet you don't like him? That doesn't make sense.'

'It does when he's got a gun at my heart. I killed a man back in Denver, and Mark saw me do it. I'd probably be up the river by now if it wasn't for his . . . protection.'

Smoke was silent for a moment, brushing crumbs from his lips and shirt. Then he gave his wide grin.

'Mebbe the jigger deserved killing — or was it an accident? I can't picture you as a calculating murderess.'

'He got fresh and attacked me, so I defended myself. I shot him — then I guess I fainted. When I came 'round I found the guy was dead. Mark helped me get away before the law caught up. Now I'm afraid to move, 'less I can find a man who's willing to take a chance on me.'

Smoke got to his feet and nursed his arm. Then he jerked his head.

'Mebbe we'd better get below to the wheel. Tarlton said something about you being on in ten minutes, didn't he? It's ways past that now.'

'He can wait,' Trixie said, with a sullen look.

She rose too, inspected herself in the mirror, and then went ahead of Smoke through the doorway. She led the way through a short passage, then emerged from behind an ornamental screen into the smoke and noise of the main gaming saloon. Smoke looked about him, noting how the place had filled up. Then Tarlton came over from his position by an ornate pillar, a cheroot smouldering between his strong teeth.

'Feelin' better?' he enquired, and it sounded as though he didn't give a damn.

'Between the beef and the girl friend, I'm on top of the world,' Smoke answered. 'Seems you found a couple of nuggets I carry around.'

'Yeah.' Tarlton inspected his fingernails. 'Since I had hold of your ankles I couldn't help but feel 'em. Sorry I probed. Sort of habit I have.'

'I'm taking a chance with them.' Smoke stooped, put his thumb in the stitches about his trouser cuff, then handed the nuggets over. 'I want five hundred for them. That's an assayer's valuation of them.'

'Okay.' Without hesitation Tarlton handed over five hundred in one-hundred bills, then his eyes strayed to Trixie. 'Did you fix up our friend like I told you?'

'I already said I liked the beef, didn't I?' Smoke asked.

'Uh-huh. And the girl. You're welcome to the beer, fella.'

There was a taut silence for a moment, then Trixie broke in:

'Since you're taking a chance with that five hundred, Smoke, you'd better get busy. I'll show you the wheel — and listen, Mark,' she added, 'I'm standing beside Smoke as his mascot, so there'll be no songs from me tonight.'

'Okay, I can't make you sing.' Tarlton merely shrugged. 'Just don't throw too much into your work, that's all. I'm not objectin' to you helping a stranger out — providing it stops there.'

With that Tarlton turned away. Smoke hesitated, his eyes hard, but much that he would have liked to have done at that moment was made impossible because he had only one sound arm and no guns. So he followed Trixie to the table and sat down, his eyes on the spinning wheel, the eager faces, and the dead pan of the croupier.

Smoke's money and chips changed hands. Trixie stood behind him, her rounded arms reaching down, and her fingers interlocking over Smoke's chest. She had a subtle persuasion about the way she did things. Smoke felt the warmth of her breathing on the back of his head.

'Six,' she whispered in his ear. 'Risk that number.'

'Okay, lady. You've bin around here

more than I have.'

Six it was. Smoke put a hundred dollars' worth of chips on the square. Silence. Curling smoke, intent faces, the rippling click of the racing ball. The wheel stopped spinning and '6' it was.

Smoke grinned and sat back, watching the winnings pushed towards him. He reached up his free hand and stroked the side of Trixie's smooth cheek gently. She pressed closer to his back, lit a cigarette and then put it between his lips. He went on playing, listening for her voice.

'Six again,' she murmured.

The wheel spun steadily. Smoke watched, the cigarette fumes curling round his half-closed eyes. '6' once more!

'I told you you needed a mascot,' Trixie said in his ear. 'And you also need a drink — Charley,' she added to the nearby waiter, 'fetch a drink. What are you having, Smoke?'

'Double brandy. I need it. And I can pay for it,' he added, grinning. 'Name

27

your own liquor, Trix.'

'Soft drink, any sort,' she told Charley, and to Smoke's surprised glance she added, 'I never touch hard liquor.'

Smoke shrugged and motioned to his pile of chips.

'Mebbe it's time I drew out?' he asked. 'I've got four times as much as when I started.'

'And four hundred not touched,' Trixie said. 'What kind of a gambler do you call yourself? Put all you've got and three hundred more on seven.'

'Seven?' Smoke looked dubious. 'Changing horses isn't such a good idea if you're on a winning streak.'

'Do as I tell you. I'm your mascot, aren't I?'

'7' came up and Smoke began laughing. This was too easy. He drank half of his double brandy, flipped across the money to the waiter, and looked up at Trixie. Her face above him seemed to be upside down and she was smiling. He went on playing steadily, and drinking. More brandy kept mysteriously replacing that which he had already had. Seven! Six! Three! Nine! There was a magical quality about the way he kept winning. Then amidst the haze he heard Trixie say:

'Fifteen, Smoke. Everything you've got.'

Without hesitation he obeyed . . . and watched No 3 come up. In fixed, bemused silence he saw everything vanish from under his hand as the rake came across the table. Ridiculous, of course. Everything couldn't go just like that. He lurched to his feet and gazed at Trixie stupidly. He could hardly see her, so powerful was the quantity of liquor he had unthinkingly consumed in his excitement.

'I — I lost,' he whispered, and she put her hands on his shoulders.

'Yes, Smoke, you lost. Just one of those things, I guess. I — I couldn't help it.'

'Get outa my way,' Smoke muttered, his voice thickening. 'Yuh same as all women, Trixie — no durned good. G'on — get out.'

He gave her a shove with his free hand and moved unsteadily amidst the tables, colliding with some of them, then straightening. He kept his wavering vision fixed on the distant batwings and had just about reeled to them when Trixie caught up with him. She caught at his waist, encircling it with her arm.

'Thought I told you to leave me alone?' Smoke glared at her.

'You can't go like this, Smoke,' she insisted. 'You're drunk for one thing — You've no guns — and no money.'

'Yore tellin' me,' he commented sourly. 'An' I don't want yuh help — '

'You're getting it just the same. I'm taking you over to Ma Bradshaw. I've a room there, too. She'll look after you.'

'I don't need a woman lookin' after me. They're out to gyp me, same as you are . . . '

Trixie did not listen. She held on to Smoke's waist and supported him as best she could as he lurched helplessly down the steps to the main street. He had not much idea what happened after that. His liquor deadened senses refused to function and everything was a chaos that made no sense . . .

Some ten minutes later Trixie returned into the saloon and found Mark Tarlton waiting for her by the batwings. He was propped up against the wall, cheroot half-consumed, a cold gleam in his dark eyes.

'Very pretty,' he said, straightening, and Trixie flashed him a look of contempt.

'I've got some human feelings even if you haven't, Mark. Though goodness knows why I should have in a den like this.'

'Stop trying to be an angel and take some advice. From now on you can stop giving the glad hand to saddle-tramps.'

'Smoke Cavendish isn't a tramp. He's got class — deep down.'

'What am I supposed to do? — start blasting? Get it through your head,

Trixie, that I won't stand for the way you're acting. Suckers come and go, but once they've left this saloon they're finished — far as you're concerned.'

Trixie was silent, her hands clenched at her sides.

'True, he was only worth five hundred dollars,' Tarlton admitted, tossing the two gold nuggets up and down in his palm. 'But even five hundred out of a saddle-tramp is better than nothing. 'And he bought plenty of liquor — or you did for him. You did nicely, Trix, but just stay in line.'

'Some day,' Trixie said deliberately, 'a guy's going to realize that that wheel of yours is fixed, then he'll come and shoot up the joint, and you with it. I hope I'm around when it happens.'

'You might even be in it,' Tarlton said drily. 'Don't stick your pretty face out too far, kid, it might get lifted quicker than you expect. And don't go forgetting, either, that there's a matter of a murder back in Denver.'

Trixie breathed hard and seemed on

the point of a violent outburst, but Tarlton checked her.

'No hard feelings,' he said, and removing his cheroot from his teeth he kissed her casually — so casually, she boiled. 'Better give the customers a song; they're waiting for it.'

Trixie swung away, her cheeks hot with anger, and headed for the rostrum where the three-piece orchestra was trying to make itself audible over the din.

2

Sledgehammers in his skull and numbness in his arm and shoulder brought Smoke out of a stupefied sleep towards dawn. For a long time he lay licking his lips and feeling as though he had been eating the blanket. Then he grunted at the pain in his head and his hand shifted to his shoulder. He kept his eyes shut and tried to figure out what had happened. By degrees he pieced it all together and his eyes opened slowly to the grey light filling the room.

He was in a comfortable bed, fully dressed, his shirt open at the neck. Only his boots had been removed. With an effort he forced himself on the elbow of his sound arm, and then he gave a start of surprise.

Coiled in a big chair in the corner was a sleeping figure. Tousled blonde hair peeped over the top of a rug she had drawn up over her shoulders. Her feet, devoid of shoes, projected from the bottom of the rug.

Grim-faced, Smoke eased himself from the bed. He looked at Trixie for a moment or two and then went across to the washbowl. Pouring water from the jug he swilled his face and the back of his neck, then experimented with the razor which had been left with him. His injured arm was devilish stiff, but deep down it felt better. Finally he pulled on his boots and shook the girl into wakefulness. The rug fell from her as she stirred. She was still in her sequinned gown.

'What's the idea, Trix?' Smoke asked briefly.

She got up from the chair quickly, glancing away, for a moment from his hard stare.

'I — I thought I'd better keep an eye on you — with that injured shoulder. So I moved in.'

'I gathered that. Considering you were dead asleep you were not much of a nurse, were you?'

'I managed to stay awake until nearly dawn.'

Smoke searched her beautiful but tired face in the waxing daylight.

'I haven't got much to thank you for,' he said finally. 'I gather you're a professional clipper.'

'Because you lost your money? I didn't fix that Smoke — cross my heart. It was Mark. The wheel's phony.'

'Which you knew about?'

'Sure thing, but I never thought he was going to spring anything last night. Usually he lets a customer get away with it the first time, then gyps him the second. I was going to see there never was a second time for you.'

'Weren't very successful, were you?' Smoke's voice was still harsh.

'Mark did it on purpose to clean you out quick. He didn't like the attention I'd been giving you.'

Smoke reflected, then turned away. He looked out of the window on the deserted, ramshackle street, fastening up his shirt collar as he did so. After a moment Trixie was holding his arm tightly.

'Smoke, look at me!' she insisted. 'Don't treat me this way! I'm all for you — with everything I've got. I wouldn't have spent the night watching over you otherwise. A woman only does that for a man she . . . loves.'

Smoke didn't say anything.

'My room is next door,' she hurried on. 'I climbed through my window and got in here. Ma Bradshaw doesn't know anything about it, and she mustn't — ever. She's tough about things like that. I paid for the room, and everything.'

Smoke turned at last, his face unsmiling.

'You're in too deep with Mark Tarlton to mean anything to me, kid,' he said briefly. 'You played the game his way last night and cleaned me out. Okay, so I was a sucker. Let it go at that. If you're looking for a man I'm not the one.'

'Smoke!' Trixie dived after him as he strode to the door. 'Smoke, you can't leave like this, after all I've done!'

'That's just the reason I am doing it. Call it a day, Trix. Be easier all round.'

He looked at her steadily. There were tears blurring her grey eyes and a forlorn droop to her mouth. For a second or two he was not sure of his judgment; then tightening his lips he pulled the door open and strode out into the narrow passage. In a moment or two he had hurried downstairs. Ma Bradshaw, accustomed to early risers, came lumbering out of the kitchen regions.

'Well, howdy Mr Cavendish! Feelin' better?' She was a big, clean woman with three chins and an outsized bosom. 'You sure had plenty of firewater away last night.'

'Yeah — a failing of mine,' Smoke answered briefly. 'Look, Ma, I've a proposition to put to you. I'm flat broke, but for one good meal I'll do any job you want.'

'With that arm? Who are yuh trying to kid? As for your breakfast, that's no worry. It's paid fur. Miss Lee saw to that. She fixed it last night.'

'Oh . . . ' Smoke found himself feeling like a two-cent heel. 'Nice of her. I'll have the breakfast right now, Ma, and then be on my way.'

Ma nodded and hurried back to the kitchen regions. Smoke wandered into the dining-room, nodding to the few punchers who were making an early start to the day. Some of them were already half-way through their breakfasts. Mooching over to a window table Smoke sat down and reflected. His eyes surveyed the main street and settled at length on a great barn of a building with a signboard outside —

FOR SALE. ONLY $8,000.

Apply Luke Bairstow,
Attorney-at-Law,
Hell's Acres.

An idea drifted through Smoke's mind, then passed on again. That building was a temptation. Bigger than the ornate Hell's Acres Saloon across the street. Suppose there came to be a second saloon in town — ? Smoke sighed and relaxed. $8,000 couldn't be plucked from a tree.

In another moment or two Ma Bradshaw brought his breakfast — a man-sized meal. He ate hungrily, drank all the coffee, and felt like a hundred per cent. when he had finished. He had just got to his feet when Trixie came in, dressed in a simple tweed skirt and blouse, her blonde hair flowing free. It made her years younger. Smoke hesitated as she came towards him.

'Thanks for the breakfast, Trix,' he said. 'One day I'll come back and pay my bill.'

He could not be sure whether it was pride, anger, or plain obstinacy which was mastering him — but whichever it was he obeyed it. Striding past the girl he went into the hallway and out on to the porch. In another moment he was marching along the boardwalk, and he kept on going until he had reached the livery stable at the end of the street.

'Yeah?' Mort Clayburn, the stable owner, as well as being blacksmith and parson, looked up from shoeing a horse. 'Somethin' I can do, stranger?'

'How far do you trust me?' Smoke asked.

'Depends. I don't reckon to distrust anybody till I've good reason. What's on your mind?'

'I want a horse to carry me to Nebraska. I've a job there, and money waiting for me — the Yellow V spread. I lost my own cayuse to side-winders only yesterday. You loan me a horse and when I've gotten to Nebraska I'll collect my money and bring the horse back — and pay for the loan.'

Clayburn reflected. 'I reckon to be a man of God, even if I do work in a place where God is just a fancy name,' he mused. 'Mebbe I like you, mebbe I'm crazy — but anyways I'll take a chance. There's a gelding there you can have.'

Smoke glanced towards the animal, then he patted Clayburn's shoulder with his free hand.

'You're regular, pardner; I won't forget it.'

'I know you won't. I kinda know who I can trust.'

Smoke turned away, took down a saddle from the rack, and threw it over the gelding. One-handedly he drew the cinches tight and then swung up with practised ease. In another moment he was riding the animal out of the stable — to find Trixie on the corner of the boardwalk looking anxiously up and down the street.

'Smoke!' she cried, as she saw him. 'Smoke, wait a minute!'

He pulled up gradually, half reluctant. The girl hurried over to him, her hands catching at his leg, her face imploring.

'Smoke, please don't leave me!' she entreated. 'You've got this whole thing mixed up. I was gypped as much as you were last night by Mark fixing that wheel . . . You've got to believe that!'

'Sorry, kid,' Smoke shook his head. 'I guess Mark's too strong an influence in your life for me to want any part of you. You didn't forget to see I got drunk, did you, so I couldn't figure things out? I'm on my way, Trix — and thanks for the bed and breakfast.'

Savagely Smoke drove in the spurs and the gelding jumped forward. Smoke could hear the girl's frantic voice shouting after him.

'Smoke, come back! Come back! You've no guns, no provisions — You can't ever make it . . . '

Then distance had killed her cries and Smoke rode on stubbornly. He thought a good deal as he did so. He knew her warnings had been correct. The spot he wanted in Nebraska was hundreds of miles away, and with no provisions and no weapons it was suicide to attempt the trip. Unless, as he hoped, he fell in with other riders headed that way who'd share their chow with him. Or at the next town he might get some kind of job to straighten him up a bit before he went on his way. Anything to get out of Hell's Acres and the reach of a girl whom he felt sure had taken him for everything he'd got.

By mid-morning he was well clear of Hell's Acres and following the resumption of the mountains which spread beyond the town and surrounding pasture land. Very much alone in the world he jogged the borrowed gelding along the narrow trail walled in by tall rock faces. The one hope in his mind was that he would hit another town before long — and certainly before night. With no bedroll or other protection night would be hell with its bitter wind —

Then the crack of a rifle shot blasted his thoughts wide open. He looked up sharply, drawing to a halt and looking about him. The shot had not been aimed at him; it had been too far away. It had come from somewhere ahead. So he rode forward again, cautiously, remembering that he had no arms of his own, and only one good fist.

After a minute or two he came round a bend in the trail, and drew to an immediate halt. Quickly he slipped from the saddle and pulled the horse into cover of the rocks, then he stood watching the scene ahead of him. Fifty yards away the trail dipped slightly and in the middle of it, hemmed in by the tall cliffs, was a group of men. Three had their backs to Smoke, and the centremost was wearing a white Stetson which had turned yellow. Beyond the trio of gunmen, his hands raised, was a fat, middle-aged man in seedy looking black clothes, his horse standing nearby. He had his hands raised and was obviously being robbed.

'The parasites,' Smoke whispered, his eyes glinting, and he wished to heaven he had the use of his wounded arm. There might be other ways though, providing he could think of something quickly.

He looked about him, then caught sight of the ears of a horse above a rock ledge not far away. It probably was one of the horses of the gunmen. Smoke got on the move immediately, well covered by the rocks, and gained the ledge in a matter of minutes. His guess had been right. Three horses were tethered to a rock spur, and one of them had a rifle fixed to the saddle.

Smoke yanked it out, put it to his shoulder, and held it with his undamaged hand, supporting the barrel on the rock in front of him. He took careful aim, and then fired. That yellow hat, so distinctive, suddenly flew through the air and the gunman looked about him wildly.

'Hold it!' Smoke yelled. 'The next one gets you in the belly if any of you move! Drop your hardware!'

The men did not obey until a second shot spat dirt away near their feet; then they dropped their guns hastily and stood watching as Smoke emerged from cover, the rifle still held at his shoulder.

'Don't think I can't fire with one hand,' he said grimly, advancing.

Evidently the one known as Jed had his doubts for he dived suddenly, then screamed with pain as a rifle bullet went clean through his palm. He straightened up again, blood pouring between the fingers of his other hand as he gripped his injured member tightly.

'I'm not kidding,' Smoke added, then to the fat man he said, 'Pick up those two guns, mister, and keep these mugs covered whilst I ditch this rifle.'

The fat man did not even hesitate. Reaching the guns on the ground Smoke picked up one of them and examined it, then he grinned and, picking up its companion, stuck it in his belt.

'Thanks for my Colts back again,' he said. 'I feel heaps better. Sort of lucky I ran into you mugs again.'

The outlaws did not respond, but their eyes were glinting over their bandannas.

'Pull off their masks, dad,' Smoke

ordered. 'Let's see who the critters are.'

The fat man nodded and the bandannas fell to the ground. Lean, cruel faces were revealed, but to Smoke none of them was recognizable, nor to the fat man to judge from the shrug he gave.

'Seems to me,' Smoke said deliberately, 'that you owe me a thousand smackers and he looked at Yellow Hat.

'Yeah? Try and get it!'

'Just what I aim to do, even if I have to kick your teeth out. Keep him covered, dad, whilst I soften him up a bit.'

Smoke put his gun beside its twin in his belt and then clenched his fist. Yellow Hat watched the movement and gave a cynical grin, satisfied he could easily get out of the way of a one-handed man. Unfortunately, as the fist slammed out, he jerked his head in the wrong direction and the knuckles crashed with shattering violence on his nose. Blood began to trickle as he recovered his balance. He did not dare hit back with guns trained on him.

'The hardware equalizes things,' Smoke explained drily. 'I'm one handed at the moment . . . How's about it? Want some more softening up or do you feel like handing over?'

Yellow Hat hesitated, then with a scowl he felt in his hip pocket and whipped out an automatic. Instantly the fat man fired. Yellow Hat gave a yelp of pain as the slug tore across his chest. He staggered, dropped the automatic, then slowly crumpled to his knees.

'Better not pull any fancy tricks,' Smoke advised, and examined the gun hawk's hip pocket quickly. Finding nothing, he examined the shirt pockets, and brought a wad of greenbacks to view. Holding them in his slinged hand he counted them quickly, and nodded.

'Satisfied?' Yellow Hat panted, hand to his wounded chest.

'Far as I'm concerned. How's about you, dad? What did these lice take from you?'

'Two hundred, son. That one with

the split hand did it.'

Smoke nodded, recovered the two hundred in a matter of moments, and handed them across. Then he eyed the three men grimly.

'I could shoot the lot of you down only I'm not a killer — and none of you are, so you say. Anyways, I never caught you out doing it . . . So I'm just leaving you to sweat. You can cut your bullet out of your chest best you know how, Yellow Hat. Okay dad, grab your horse. We'll be on our way.'

The fat man picked up the remaining guns and stuck them in his belt, then catching at his horse's reins he followed Smoke out of the gully and finally to the point where Smoke had left his horse.

'I'm Smoke Cavendish,' Smoke said, as the fat man gave him a questioning glance.

'Glad to know you, boy. You saved my life . . . I'm Brady Carmichael, of Des Moines, Iowa. Some folks call me 'One Shot'.'

'Yeah?' Smoke looked at him. 'Good with the hardware, you mean?'

'Heck, no. With a gambling wheel. I'm a professional.'

Smoke was silent, studying the man. He was round-faced and genial with pink cheeks, laughing blue eyes, and grey hair peeping at the sides of his Stetson. He looked like a man who could take life or leave it and never get ruffled. But a professional gambler — !

'Where are you headed?' Smoke asked abruptly.

'I was on my way to Topeka until those coyotes set about me. Come to think of it I'm still on my way there, thanks to you. From what I hear of the place there's easy pickings.'

'I know somewheres where they're easier. Let's ride on a bit and I'll explain as we go. Those mugs are too close for comfort.'

Smoke nodded towards the gunmen, where they could see two of them busy tending their wounds with the help of the uninjured third man; then he swung

51

up to his saddle and urged his horse forward. In a moment or two Brady Carmichael had caught up with him.

'Seems to me you're going the wrong way, fella,' Carmichael said. 'You musta been goin' the opposite direction to catch up on me the way you did.'

'I was — but I've changed my mind.' Smoke's lips were tight. 'I've just remembered some unfinished business — same kinda place as where you can get easy pickings. Tell me something, One Shot: do you play straight or crooked?'

'What kind of a question is that?' Carmichael hooted.

'A necessary one — and I don't want any funny answers.'

'Okay, I play straight. Give me a wheel that isn't fixed — and that's a mighty rare thing around here — and I guess there ain't a chance on God's earth for the banker.'

Smoke grinned to himself but did not comment. In fact he kept turning matters over in his mind for the next couple of miles, then as a water-hole loomed up he dismounted, and Carmichael did likewise.

'I've no chow,' Smoke said, 'but I see you have. Mind if I borrow some?'

'After your saving my life? Have what you want.'

They settled down together, the horses busy at the water-hole. From the look of things it was around noon and the sun was blistering down from the cloudless sky. Smoke cuffed up his hat and regarded the sweating Carmichael.

'I've a matter to square in Hell's Acres,' he said. 'Ever hear of it?'

'Nope.'

'It's the name of a town and a saloon. The saloon's run by a guy named Mark Tarlton who seems to have the sole control. Last night a dame who works for him, a clipper, got me drunk and saw to it that I was gypped of several thousand dollars. I want it back. I'm a gambler, but not a professional — an' I can't beat a wheel which is fixed.'

'Well?' Carmichael asked, lighting a cheroot.

'I figgered you and me might go back to Hell's Acres, try and rustle up some boys who feel like we do, and make Tarlton use a straight wheel. You could take him for all he's got, mebbe.'

'No mebbe about it. Sounds like a nice idea. But what do you get out of it? You won't be playing with my money, will you?'

'No. You'll be playing for me. I'm doing a deal with you, One Shot. I saved your life, and I reckon that's worth a reward. You got any more money with you besides that two hundred those outlaws took?'

Carmichael grinned. 'Sure thing. I've two rolls of notes stuffed in my boot heels . . . ' and he stretched out his feet to reveal the high-heeled riding boots he was wearing. 'I guess there'll be around two thousand there.'

Smoke looked at him steadily. 'Feel like gambling one thousand on my account? If you're as good as you say you are I'm worth the investment. I can pay it back out of the winnings.'

For a long time Carmichael thought it out, cheroot smoke drifting into his eyes; then finally he gave a nod.

'Okay, I'll risk it — but only on condition that that wheel is running true. I'm playing no game if it's fixed.'

'When we get back into town I'll rustle up what boys I can to help us,' Smoke said, 'and then we'll have a showdown. Time I got this infernal arm of mine back in action, too.'

He withdrew it gently from the sling and, wincing, straightened it out gradually. He felt the torn flesh pull savagely, but the hurt was not so vicious as he had expected. Pulling the sling away he studied it for a moment. He had never noticed before that it had a lace edge.

'Woman's?' Carmichael asked, with a grin.

'Yeah — the one that took me for everything.' Smoke bundled the sling up and threw it on the ground, then he sat musing with his mouth tight.

'Suppose you win several thousand dollars, fella, what good does it do you?' Carmichael asked. 'Do you aim to drift on somewheres else afterwards?'

'No. I figger that if I can win around ten thousand I'll have enough to buy a deserted building opposite Tarlton's saloon, and also have enough to live on for a while.'

'Deserted building? How much good will that do you?'

'Plenty. I aim to open in opposition to Tarlton. He's had his own way too long in Hell's Acres. You might even like to be in on the deal?'

'Mebbe. On the other hand, son, mebbe I'm too much of a wanderer . . . See how things make out.'

Smoke got to his feet. 'I guess we may as well be on our way,' he said. 'Nothing to hang around here for.'

Carmichael nodded and heaved his obese body upwards, then Smoke headed for his nearby horse.

3

Smoke deliberately delayed arrival in Hell's Acres until nightfall. He wanted to avoid attracting too much notice, and for another he did not wish to be bothered by Trixie — so it was an hour after sundown when he and Carmichael rode into town, dismounting when they had reached the livery stable. Mort Clayburn was within — not working — but on hand in case any horses were needed. He looked up in surprise as Smoke came into range of the oil lamps.

'Hello there, fella — thought you'd hit leather for other parts. What brought you back?'

'Business,' Smoke answered. 'Here's the horse you loaned me — and many thanks. I've decided to stick around for a bit. I'll pay you for the horse's hire soon as I can get some money together.'

'Forget it.'

Smoke hesitated for a moment and then continued: 'I don't have to wonder if you're a square-shooter, Clayburn; you've already proved it by the way you've helped me. I've a plan in which you might be interested. I aim to make Mark Tarlton use an unfixed wheel at his gaming table for perhaps the first time in his life.'

'That will be something,' Clayburn smiled. 'If you can do it. Tarlton has the town right behind him, remember. He owns most of it. I don't think one man like yourself is going to make him change his ways.'

'I've a professional gambler right here who can make any straight spinning wheel do just what he wants,' Smoke went on, with a nod towards Carmichael. 'How thoroughly we can deal with Tarlton and make him act straight depends on you, me, and whatever other fellows we can dig up.'

'Me?' Clayburn looked astonished. 'I'm no gunman — and I never go in

Tarlton's place, either. Hardly do since I'm a minister. Church and Tarlton don't mix.'

'It's not a case of church and Tarlton; it's a case of right and wrong. Tarlton's had too much of his own way around here for too long, from what I can judge. I aim to alter it — but I need help. Since you stand for the right you're the man to help. How many guys can you rustle up to see my way of thinking?'

'Well — a dozen mebbe. I can tell you better in an hour. I'll have to contact them.'

'Okay, do that. Bring them here and let me talk to 'em. We'll look after your stable whilst you go, in case anybody needs anything.'

Clayburn nodded and, evidently having decided to help, he departed into the kerosene-lighted street outside. Smoke settled down to wait, Carmichael beside him — and at length, by ones and twos, men began to arrive, until finally there was a good dozen of them, including Clayburn himself.

Smoke explained the situation just as he had done so to Clayburn, and when he had finished the men glanced at one another.

'I reckon it's a mighty good idea,' one of them said. 'I guess there isn't a man or woman in this town that hasn't been double-crossed in some way by Tarlton. He owns too durned many things — general stores, barber's, the saloon, and one or two small joints. He can charge what he likes and do what he likes. Only law there is belongs to him, and the mayor and sheriff are greased to do lip-service to him.'

'Which is going to change,' Smoke said decisively, getting to his feet. 'What he needs is to be taught how to play a straight game, and also what stiff competition means. Okay, I'm relying on you men to back me up in my plans.'

'Sure thing.'

'We'll do that, Smoke.'

'And when do you propose doing

something?' Clayburn asked.

'Tonight. No reason why not. If we wait until tomorrow Tarlton will get to know I'm back in town and that may spoil my surprise. I'm ready to lead this little party of mine straight into the saloon and demand a new deal at the gaming table. We'll probably win plenty to our side by the stand we'll make. So far, Tarlton's had no opposition, but he's sure going to get it now.'

The men glanced at each other and then nodded, their expressions grim.

'No killing,' Smoke warned. 'I'll not stand for that. We want a straight deal — not murder. How's about you, One Shot? If we can get a straight wheel do you think you're in the mood to play?'

'I'm always in the mood,' Carmichael grinned, and screwed back the left heel on his half-boot. 'And here's the money — or half of it, anyways.'

He held it up, then put it in his pocket. 'But how do you figger getting mixed up in some tough dealing with that arm of yours?' he asked.

'It'll stand it. Time it got hardened out. All right,' Smoke added, 'let's go.'

He led the way out of the livery stable, his right hand on the butt of the gun in his belt. He would have preferred his holsters for quick drawing, but at the moment had none. Without pause, the men and Carmichael coming behind him, he walked the street, ascended the three steps outside the Hell's Acres, and then pushed open the batwings. His actual entry only attracted casual glances at first, then the looks became more attentive as the dozen or so men came in behind him, all of them with their hands on their guns. It was quite the most businesslike deputation that had ever walked into Tarlton's undisputed territory.

At the far end of the saloon, on the rostrum, Trixie Lee was in the midst of a song. She broke off half-way as she recognized Smoke through the tobacco haze; then she made a dive to the floor, pushing her way amidst the tables.

'Smoke! It's you!' she cried, as she

came nearer, her eyes bright. 'You've come back — '

'But not for you, Trix.' Smoke cut her short and aimed a grim glance. 'Better put yourself somewheres safe, kid: there may be trouble. I'm here to make amends for last night.'

'Against Mark?' she asked, startled. 'You're crazy, Smoke. You'll never get away with it.'

Smoke did not answer her. His eyes were fixed on Mark Tarlton himself as he came slowly across the saloon. As usual he was perfectly dressed, his white shirt front gleaming, his hair polished. He took the cheroot from his teeth as he came up, but despite his broad smile his eyes were wary.

'Back in town, eh, Smoke? Thought you'd started for Nebraska.'

'Hoped I had, you mean.' Smoke fixed him with a look. 'I had a change of heart. I'm back to collect what's owing to me.'

'Owing?'

'The money you frisked last night on

63

that damned roulette wheel of yours. You and your girl friend Trix had nice pickings — but now mebbe it's my turn.'

Tarlton's dark eyes travelled over the man at the rear of Smoke, and finally to Clayburn.

'What's the parson doing here?' Tarlton asked. 'Thought a man of God wouldn't defile himself by coming in this den of liquor.'

'I'll come anywhere where wrong wants righting,' Clayburn retorted.

'Yeah? What do you want me to do? — take up Bible lessons?'

There was a chuckle from the men at the nearby tables and Tarlton grinned widely.

'You're on my property, fellas,' he said, 'and that gives me the right to order you off it. So blow before I get the sheriff and his boys to work.'

Abruptly Smoke had his gun out. His face was taut.

'This is no social call, Tarlton. You've a job to do — Get all the players from that gaming table of yours and let us examine that wheel — at close quarters.'

Tarlton's grin vanished. 'You're crazy? You can't come in here an' accuse me of — '

'I can, and I'm doing it. You've gypped once too often, Tarlton, and I'm changing things. Go on — get your players away, and your damned croupier and the rest of 'em.'

Tarlton began to back, menaced by the gun. He glanced about him anxiously, but his own men scattered about the saloon did not act for fear Smoke might get in a fatal shot before succumbing to one himself.

At last the table was reached, but Tarlton did not give any order. Instead he took a chance and slammed up his fist clean to Smoke's jaw. He took it full on and reeled backwards, hitting a chair and collapsing across it. Instantly Tarlton whipped out his gun, then dropped it as the minister — blacksmith slashed up a haymaker. Dazed,

Tarlton crashed on to the gaming table, sending money and chips in all directions. Not satisfied with this the blacksmith whirled Tarlton up again, then banged his head down time and again with vicious impact on the green baize covering.

'Stop, you durned fool!' Tarlton yelled. 'Yore killing me — !'

Another concussion blasted through his skull, then Smoke's gun was in his ribs. He straightened up slowly, his head singing.

'Okay, okay,' he whispered. 'The game's off, folks. This loco saddle-tramp here wants the wheel examined. Let him do it: I can't argue on this end of the hardware.'

Smoke signalled briefly and his men went to work to upend the table. In a matter of seconds they discovered the wire and roller-brake device which controlled the wheel by pressure from the croupier's foot. Those who had been playing looked at each other, then at Tarlton. Their eyes were glinting dangerously and Smoke read the signs.

'There'll be no lynch law here,' he said curtly. 'It surprises me some of you regulars didn't know this wheel was fixed. How else do you think this mug has made enough money to own half the town?'

'I'll make you damned well fry for this before I'm through, Cavendish,' Tarlton breathed, his fists clenched.

'Make sure it isn't yourself. The folks here aren't so happy about you from the looks of them . . . I've no legal right to kick you out of town, even though I'd like to — but you sure will play straight from here on. Okay, fellas,' Smoke added, 'tear out those wires and put the wheel back. Let's have a straight deal for once.'

Without hesitation his instructions were obeyed and the wires flung to a distant corner of the saloon. Then the wheel was planted back in position. Smoke glanced around him on the grim faces.

'Who's the sheriff in this dump?' he

asked, and a thin, hatchet-faced man with a cleft chin came forward.

'I am,' he growled. 'So what?'

'So this! You're supposed to dispense law an' order around here, but the way I figger it you don't. You lick Tarlton's boots and let it go at that. You've got to mend your ways, sheriff.'

'Who says so?'

'I do — on behalf of all right-thinking people here. You've seen what Tarlton's been pulling — and there's a penalty for it. What are you going to do about it?'

'Nothing!' the sheriff spat. 'I'm taking no orders from a saddle-tramp. Best thing you can do is to get to hell outa here, and take these mugs who follow you along with you.'

Smoke eyed him, then asked another question: 'Where's the mayor?'

A small, pot-bellied man came forward from the assembly, a sombrero pushed to the back of his head. He was shiny, pinch-eyed, and from the look of him thoroughly unreliable.

'Only one man can depose the sheriff and put in another man,' Smoke told him. 'And that man's you — '

'Depose nothin'!' the sheriff roared. 'What in tarnation are yuh talking about, Cavendish? I'm sheriff around here and I — '

'Shut up!' Smoke glanced at him in contempt. 'You're only sheriff by the vote of the people — and most of them are in this saloon right now. We'll take a vote on it and see if they still want you to dispense law and order. All right, folks, what about it? How many of you want this sheriff to stay right where he is!'

About a dozen hands went up, mostly from men at the back of the hall who were obviously Tarlton's stooges and therefore did not dare vote any other way.

'Now — how many for a change of sheriff?' Smoke asked.

It seemed that nearly every remaining hand went up, men and women included. Smoke grinned and looked at the scowling Tarlton.

'Looks like you lost your chief 'Yes-man' Tarlton,' he remarked drily. 'Let's see who replaces him . . . Up to you, folks,' Smoke went on. 'You've heard me called a saddle-tramp, an interferin' guy, and other things — but at least I've exposed part of the rottenness corrupting this town. I'll carry it further if I can get the law on my side backing me up. I'm putting up as sheriff, and naming the parson — blacksmith here as my chief deputy. How's about it?'

'You got yuhself a job, Smoke!'

'Yeah, sure! Kick out that other blasted tinbadge!'

'Get busy, mayor, and swear him in.'

The mayor mopped his face and gave Tarlton a look to receive a stony glare in return. But the mayor was in a position from which he could not retreat — so he performed the brief ceremony, tugged the star badge from the shirt of the angry sheriff, and handed it to Smoke. With a nod Smoke put the badge in his pocket for the moment.

'By tomorrow this badge is going to be sewn on good and tight,' he said, 'and later on, mayor, I'll square up the matter of my pay for this job — '

'I can sew your badge on, Smoke!'

Smoke turned and found he was looking at Trixie's earnest face. She had that entreating look in her grey eyes as she came forward from amidst the crowd.

'I'm making a clean sweep, Trix,' he told her. 'That includes everything and everybody connected with Tarlton . . . Okay, you folks,' he continued, turning his back on the girl, 'start making your game. And this time it won't be crooked. I don't intend stopping Tarlton running his saloon, just as long as he keeps it straight.'

'Nice of you,' Tarlton said bitterly.

'And I'm overlooking earlier double-crosses with this — and in other directions,' Smoke added. 'I wasn't sheriff then; but from here on watch your step.'

Mark Tarlton said nothing. With sombre eyes he watched the men and women resuming their positions at the table. Among them was Carmichael who settled in his chair with the air of a man about to enjoy himself. He bought his chips from the uncomfortable-looking banker and then the play began.

From the very first moment Carmichael revealed that he knew exactly what he was about. How he did it — whether it was a system, uncanny judgment, or just sheer luck — was beyond explanation, but the fact remained that as time advanced his pile of chips began to grow. All personal animosities were forgotten, even by Tarlton and Smoke, as they watched the fat man's playing. He himself seemed the least worried of anybody. He drew at his cheroot, sweated freely, and played deliberately. After two hours of play the banker withdrew and came round to Tarlton's side.

'I guess we're cleaned out, Mr

Tarlton. I need more money.'

'You're not getting it,' Tarlton snapped. 'I'm closing the game for tonight. Give that fat swine time to get on his way. The whole thing's a fix, if you ask me.'

'I don't reckon it is, boss,' the banker said. 'That fat guy plays straight. I guess he's a professional. Some of 'em work to mathematical systems and he seems t'have a good one.'

Tarlton turned away in disgust and Smoke grinned as he watched him go, then he glanced at Carmichael. 'How's about it, dad?' he asked. 'Game's finished. Feel like hitting the hay?'

'Sure thing . . . ' Carmichael changed his chips for money and then surged to his feet. Breathing heavily and stuffing notes in his pockets he came round to where Smoke was standing. 'Time you an' me and the boys had a drink,' he said. 'Come on.'

They headed towards the bar and the men and women who had been watching the game broke up. As he drank the whisky Carmichael had ordered for him, Smoke asked a question.

'How'd you make out, dad? Get that ten thousand I'd hoped for?'

'I got thirty,' Carmichael grinned. 'When you said easy pickings you weren't kidding, fella. I'll hang around this town for a while and see if I can't take Tarlton for a few more rides. In the meantime in return for the easy pickings I'll spring you fifteen thousand instead of ten. That should start you up nicely in that joint you're figgerin' on.'

'That's the nicest thing any pardner ever did for me,' Smoke said seriously. 'Why don't you come in with me? A lot of the boys will, I expect . . . ' And Smoke looked at them lined along the bar, talking amongst themselves.

'Not me, son. I'm not tying myself down to any place in partic'lar. I like to make money as I travel, not stuck in one place . . . As for the cut I'm giving you, you only owe one thousand, the original amount I staked for you. The rest is your winnings.'

'You'll get all of it back before I'm

through,' Smoke said, and his eyes showed he meant it. 'I couldn't have gotten a red cent but for you . . . '

The puncher not far from Smoke's elbow finished his drink and then edged a little closer, casually lighting a cigarette and apparently disinterested in everything around him.

'Sure that you're making the right move, son?' Carmichael asked. 'Tarlton may have been caught out with his fixed wheel, but I guess he'll see to it from here on that he doesn't step out of line. He might get lead in him if he does. That being so I reckon his saloon will have a far stronger pull than any you can put up.'

'It's worth a try,' Smoke responded. 'I aim to clean up plenty in this town and that's going to swing most of the folks over to my side. In fact, I'll make Tarlton's name smell before I'm through — and incidentally, if you're looking for a place to stay you can't do better than take Ma Bradshaw's across the street.'

'I'll remember that,' Carmichael said.

'Which just about clears up everything to date,' Smoke decided. 'I'll go and see Luke Bairstow tomorrow morning and close the deal for that place across the way.'

'You planning to stay at Ma Bradshaw's too?'

Smoke's eyes strayed to where Trixie was seated at a distant table, a soft drink in front of her. She was watching him steadily but her relaxed expression gave no indication of her thoughts.

'Yeah,' he said finally. 'Several reasons why I'd rather not, but it happens to suit me — Mebbc we'd better get over there with the boys right now, then we can square off the money.'

Carmichael nodded and at the same moment the nearby puncher drifted casually away. Trixie moved her eyes from Smoke and watched the puncher instead. After a moment or two she rose and followed him and was just in time to see him vanish inside Mark Tarlton's office.

Tarlton looked up with a scowl from

his desk as the puncher came in.

'Well? What in tarnation do you want?'

'I just picked up some news, boss, and I thought you'd like t'hear it. Smoke Cavendish is buyin' that joint across the street and aims to turn it inter a saloon — just to give yuh a run fur yuh money, far as I can figger.'

Tarlton's eyes narrowed. 'He is, huh? Dead sure on this?'

'Yeah. That fat guy who cleaned you out is loanin' him the money.'

Tarlton reflected. 'Okay, thanks. I'll tell Bairstow in the meantime how he's gotta act. If Cavendish can buy that building by the time I've finished he'll be a magician.'

The puncher grinned, turned to the door, and departed. He failed to notice Trixie's disappearance at the corner of the short passage. She for her part went straight to her dressing-room and began to change quickly. She had almost finished and was in her tweed skirt and white blouse when the door opened and Tarlton came in. He eyed her coldly as he shut the door.

'What's the idea?' he snapped. 'I've been lookin' for you. The customers want a song; 'bout time they had one; you've done precious little all evening except make a play for our new pretty-boy sheriff.'

'Next time you come in here, Mark, try knocking,' Trixie said, fastening the back of her blouse.

'I never did and never shall. What's the idea of walking out like this? What do you think I pay you for?'

'You pay me so I'll stick around — not because I'm a good singer. I've had enough of it, and I quit! Right now!'

Trixie finished fastening her blouse, took down the light dust-coat from its peg, and then moved to the door. Tarlton remained against it, his powerful arms folded.

'Chasing the Boy Scout, I suppose?' he asked drily.

'No.' Trixie looked at him frankly.

'I'm going home, that's all — to Ma Bradshaw's, and I'm not coming back here. After the way your name was kicked around this evening I'm not working for you any more. I'm particular.'

'You can't afford to be, Trixie — not with a murder rap hanging over you. Or mebbe you forgot all about that?'

'I haven't forgotten anything, and I'm going. I'll be in in the morning for my money to date.'

Tariton half raised one of his hands as though he intended to slap her savagely across the face, then apparently thinking better of it he relaxed and took his wallet from his pocket. He handed her her money deliberately.

'All right, kid, if that's the way you want it. I hope you won't live to regret it.'

She took the money, folded it into her hand, then seized the door knob. She fully expected Tarlton would try and stop her, but instead he let her go. Vaguely she wondered why. It was not like Mark Tarlton to let anything he valued slip out this easily.

Without any trouble she left the saloon and crossed the street to Ma Bradshaw's. Going through the hall into the kitchen regions she spoke to Ma Bradshaw herself.

'Yore back early, gal,' Ma Bradshaw said, in surprise. 'Anythin' wrong?'

'No, I wouldn't say that. I just decided to quit working for Tarlton, that's all. He was exposed before everybody tonight as a no-account double-crosser.'

'That ain't no surprise,' Ma commented. 'He's always bin a down critter — '

'Have you got Mr Cavendish back here?' Trixie broke in urgently.

'Matter of fact I have, and another guy — a fat one — by the name of Carmichael. Why? You wantin' to pay for Mr Cavendish again? If so, you needn't. He's in the money from the look of things.'

'I just want a word with him, that's

all. Is he in his room? Same one as before?'

'Sure he is — but y'know my regulations, gal.'

'I'm ignoring them this time, Ma. I've got to see him.'

With that Trixie swung away, hurried along the hall and then up the staircase. Reaching the door of Smoke's room she knocked sharply.

'Yeah — come in,' Smoke's voice invited.

Trixie entered. An oil lamp was glowing on the table. Smoke himself was sprawled on the bed, cigarette smouldering at the corner of his mouth, his hands behind his head. He glanced round and then gave a start. Quickly he sat up.

'What do you want?' he snapped. 'I thought it was Ma with my supper. It's on its way up.'

Trixie shut the door and came forward. Smoke got to his feet, his blue eyes fixed on her.

'I asked a question, Trix!'

'I heard you, and it's about time you realized that I'm not going to be kicked around by you any longer! All I've done so far is try and help you and you've done nothing but push me around, and I've had enough.'

'That all you came to tell me?'

'No. I came to tell you that Mark Tarlton is fixing it so that you'll not be able to buy that empty building you're counting on. I made it my business to find it out. A puncher overheard you talking to the fat man and I overheard the puncher talking to Mark. It's as simple as that.'

Smoke hesitated. The perfectly frank look in the girl's grey eyes was giving him that two-cent heel feeling again.

'Now knock me down,' she invited. 'Kick me down the stairs and rub my face in the dirt. Show what a man you are where a woman's concerned!'

The faintest glimmer of tears in her eyes at his completely unyielding attitude, she turned back to the door, but before Trixie could open it Smoke grasped her arm gently.

'Just a minute, Trix,' he murmured. 'Not so fast. Mebbe I got things figgered wrong some place.'

'Maybe!' she echoed.

'Here — sit down.' He pulled up a chair and then seated himself opposite her. 'Seems to me you'd have no cause for trying to double-cross me in a matter like this — and it also seems that you've taken one hell of a risk to find the information.'

'So much so I've quit working for Mark,' Trixie said quietly. 'I want to work with you instead: I feel safer. You're a sheriff now, and that gives protection from the law if it ever catches up with me.'

'Meaning the Denver murder rap? As to that, Trix, I can't help you if the law does catch up — unless something can prove the murder was an accident.'

'Right now,' she said, 'I've changed my horses. Before I had only Mark to rely on for protection — such as it was, but now I want to be with you. What more do you want? I've shown I'm all for you in dozens of ways — and this information I've brought you should clinch it. Honest, I never did try and gyp you. Loving you as I do I'd be an idiot to do that.'

Smoke grinned slowly. 'One thing I do like about you, kid, you don't wrap anything up. You love me — just like that!'

She was silent, studying him in that intense way she had. Then following a tap on the door Mrs Bradshaw entered with supper on a tray. She set it down on the small table and then stood with her hands on her hips, surveying the two.

'Like I sed downstairs, Trixie, this is against regulations,' she remarked.

'It's business, Ma,' Smoke said. 'And don't forget I'm the sheriff. I can order this interview if I want, and if you make me, I will — Only that wouldn't be like Ma Bradshaw.'

She smiled. 'Okay — I guess I can

trust yuh. I've put some supper in your room, Trixie.'

With that she went out and Smoke looked at the girl seriously.

'You've convinced me, Trix,' he said. 'But tagging along with me won't be any picnic. After I've bought that building there'll be nothing but hard work — '

'But you won't be able to buy it! That's the whole point! Mark's out to block you — and he can. Luke Bairstow's a big friend of his.'

'That won't help him when he's at the business end of a six-gun, Trix. The law says that he's offered that building for sale, and that means he has got to accept a buyer if one comes along. Nothing can alter that, except Mark Tarlton himself buying the building, and I can't see him doing that . . . I'll fix Bairstow, don't you worry.'

'I hope you can.' Trixie looked worried. 'I don't think you know yet how deep in you're getting. Mark wields a tremendous lot of power around here.'

'I can wield more, as sheriff — and I shall. Now don't you think you ought to be getting along to your room? You're tired. We'll talk in the morning.'

Trixie nodded, satisfied for the moment. As she rose Smoke did likewise.

'Honest, Smoke, about that gamble you made. I didn't — '

He kissed her and smiled. 'Forget it, Trix. I got the wrong end of the horse. Be mighty different from here on.'

He opened the door for her and watched her go into the corridor. When she glanced back towards his room he had withdrawn into it. Smiling happily to herself she entered her own room, struck a lucifer, and lighted the oil lamp. Then as she turned in readiness to hang up her coat she gave a violent start.

Mark Tarlton was seated in the wicker chair beside the open window, watching her steadily.

'Mark!' she gasped. 'You — you frightened me!'

'You must have a guilty conscience, honey' he commented, with a cynical grin. 'I came in through the window, just after Ma Bradshaw had been in and left your supper. You didn't think you were going to leave me that easily, did you? Where the heck have you bin all this time, anyways?'

'I — er — '

'Don't tell me. With the Tin Badge, I guess. Fallen hard for that saddle-tramp, haven't you?'

'He isn't a saddle-tramp!' Trixie retorted, fully in control of herself again. 'He's the squarest shooter I have ever met in this bullet-riddled dump.'

Mark got to his feet and eyed the girl quizzically. Then he said: 'Y'know, Trix, it's a good thing I've an amiable disposition, otherwise I might have gotten sore at the way you tried to leave me tonight.'

'No 'tried' about it. I did! And I meant it!'

'And instead want to be friendly with the man who can send you up the river, or — even worse — get you executed?'

'What in the world do you mean?' Trixie gave a blank look as she sank to a chair.

'Just this . . . Why do you think our mysterious friend knows the law so well? Why do you think he's so sure he can pump law and order into this town? Why do think he knows all the legal angles? Because he's a law officer . . . and from Denver. That suggest anything to you?'

Trixie's lower lip trembled a little. 'It's fantastic, Mark! I don't believe it.'

'Pretending to be a saddle-tramp is an old stunt of a law officer. I can tell you he's dynamite. He's around here for only one reason — to dig enough evidence out of you to nail you down. Until he can do it he's setting himself up as a tough, law-abiding citizen. That the kind of man you want to play around with?'

'I couldn't be that far wrong in my judgement!' Trixie insisted. 'He's no law officer. He's a — '

She paused, her attention drawn by Mark's hand. He was holding it out steadily and in the palm lay a marshal's badge. Deliberately he turned it over and she read the inscription:

Grant Caldwell — 3/75665
Denver City, N. Division.

'Grant Caldwell — otherwise Smoke Cavendish,' Tarlton said, and gave a hard smile.

Trixie looked up sharply. 'Where did you find this badge?'

'It was sewn in his pants. I found it when he was lying out flat in my office. You know how I snoop. I didn't say anything to you because as long as you stayed beside me I figgered I could beat anything that monkey tried to pull, but now you look like going overboard for him completely I've got to act. That's on the level, Trixie: you're making a play for a marshal and he'll nail you the instant he thinks he's got you where he wants you.'

Trixie mused for a moment or two. 'He must have missed this badge.'

'No doubt of it, and he probably suspects I've got it. But he can't go around asking for it without giving himself away, can he? Now you know why I got him drunk and cleaned up all his money. I wanted him to go out of town and then I'd have my boys take care of him. Instead, you had to make him comfortable!'

Tarlton tossed the badge up and down in his palm, then put it in his pocket.

'Up to you, Trixie. Stay with him until he blasts you wide open — or stay with me and I'll find a way to beat him. Even rub him out — accidentally.'

'I — I don't know what to think,' Trixie muttered, her brows knitted. 'He's so — so completely on the level — or seems it.'

'Just training. Fact remains you can't afford to take chances. I'll forget tonight if you come back to me. And I guess you will. I'll expect you as usual at the saloon tomorrow evening. Give you plenty of time to think it over — and don't give that chiselling mug a chance to start worming his way into your confidence.'

Tarlton gave the girl his roughly casual kiss, then he went out by the window and closed it behind him. Trixie hardly heard him go. The news had half-stunned her.

4

When Trixie did not appear in the dining-hall the following morning Smoke did not worry unduly: he imagined that the girl was sleeping late and let it go at that. He had Carmichael for company — and he also had plenty on his mind. Beside his own personal affairs, he had taken on the duties of sheriff and must, of necessity, play his role thoroughly.

Immediately after breakfast he roped in Clayburn, the blacksmith-parson — he being the first deputy — and walked with him over to the sheriff's office. Carmichael did not accompany them: he lived only by night. The day he spent in just plain walking around, or sitting reading.

The sheriff's office was bolted and barred — but it did not stay that way for long. The mayor knew his job well enough, and was anxious to hold it, so he turned up with the key and opened it. When Smoke had fixed his wage the mayor departed again, and looked glad to go.

'Right now I'm not interested in this hole,' Smoke said, surveying the smoky little place with its faded walls and endless stacks of untidy files. 'Can't be any need for all this junk in a town this size, anyways. I guess we might clear it up later and start again — meantime we've work to do. With Bairstow for instance, and be ready for trouble.'

The blacksmith looked surprised as he followed Smoke to the door.

'Trouble? Why should there be? Bairstow's a shyster, sure, like the rest of 'em — but he isn't dangerous.'

'He'll try and stop me buying that place across the road — at Mark Tarlton's orders. That's a certainty. But I guess I can handle him.'

Somewhat mystified, the blacksmith shrugged and followed Smoke along the boardwalk to the lawyer's office. Apparently he had only just arrived for his roll-top desk had not even been opened. He glanced round from studying a sheaf of papers as Smoke and Clayburn came in.

'Howdy, sheriff. Howdy, Clayburn,' he said briefly.

He was a fairly tall man with acid features and sagging lines at the corners of his mouth. His hair was thin and grey, his eyes sharp.

'You don't seem much surprised at finding me the new sheriff,' Smoke told him, cuffing up his hat. 'Not a flicker of your baby eyelashes!'

'You're wearing the badge, aren't you? And I heard that Crawley had been replaced.'

'Who told you? — Tarlton? It isn't generally known yet that I'm the new law man around here. Only those in the saloon last night heard it.'

Bairstow put down the papers with an emphatic thump.

'S'pose we get down to business?' he suggested. 'What do you want of me, sheriff? If you're checking up you'll find everything square and legal.'

'Yeah? I'll admit that when I've studied things for a week or two, certainly not right now. I don't see how anybody could be square and legal with Mark Tarlton back of him.'

'I've nobody back of me,' Bairstow snapped. 'I know the law and I practise it. And I don't like your attitude! It's a sheriff's job to co-operate, not go around shouting his face off.'

'You mean you'd like one like Crawley who was just a stooge with a star on his chest? Sorry, Bairstow, I'm not made that way. Anyways. I'm not snooping — yet. I want to do a deal and buy that empty building down the street. You're asking eight thousand. I'll give you five.'

'It wouldn't matter to me if you gave eighty-five. You're a bit too late. I sold it last night.'

'To whom?' Smoke asked deliberately. 'And think carefully before you answer.'

'I don't need to think. It isn't ethical

for me to say who my client is. You should know that as a sheriff.'

'And as a lawyer you should know that as long as that sale board is up you're ready to accept a price. If you'd sold, the board should have come down.'

'I didn't have time — '

'Don't hand me that, Bairstow. You made the sale last night, you said. You've had about twelve hours.'

Bairstow hesitated and for a moment or two Smoke eyed him steadily. Then he said:

'My offer's five thousand, Bairstow. If you can show me a deed of sale whereby that property is really sold to somebody else I'll do no more about it, because I can't. But if you can't produce a deed of sale I'm holding you to the law — which is to accept an offer when it's made to you. If you wonder what sort of law I'm talking about I mean this . . .'

Smoke's Colt came into view suddenly and he added drily: 'I reckon it's the only sort of law known around here. If I was trying to make you sign that property away to me and not offering to pay for it I'd deserve running outa town — but I'm not acting that way. Quit stalling, Bairstow,' Cavendish snapped abruptly. 'Tarlton's told you to hold out on me — I know that. You can obey him, and mebbe get a bullet, or do as I say and get five thousand.'

Not at all sure of the man he was dealing with, beyond the fact that he obviously meant business, the lawyer hesitated. Then he said lamely:

'It isn't my property. I'll have to see if the owner will sell.'

'Who is the owner?' Smoke played with his gun casually.

'Mark Tarlton. He owns half the high street.'

Smoke grinned. 'I guessed as much, which makes it just lovely. Selling to me so I can kick the props from under his clip joint. Legally I guess he can withdraw his building from offer — only he hasn't been quick enough. The board is still there; you can see it through the window. I'm buying it, Bairstow, at five thousand. And you don't have to ask Tarlton if he'll take it, either!'

The money in greenbacks slapped on the top of the roll-top and the lawyer looked at it worriedly.

'I'm acting against his orders,' he declared.

'Who do you like best, Bairstow? Yourself, or Tarlton? Act on his behalf and I'll find ways and means, in my capacity as sheriff, to expose every double-crossing deal you've ever made — and don't think I can't. No doors are barred to me, remember: this badge says as much. If you prefer to act for yourself you're safe, unless you pull something really dirty.'

'Okay,' Bairstow muttered. 'I guess you got the drop on me. But I can't take five thousand. Eight's the price.'

'I said five, and even that's robbery. Get the deed made out.'

The lawyer took a glance at the gun, at Smoke's grim face, and then hesitated no more. He filled out a ready stamped and printed form and after studying it carefully — and failing to spot any twists — Smoke signed it. Then he held out his hand.

'I'll take the key,' he said. 'Or maybe the door will just fall in?'

Bairstow handed the key over and without another word Smoke left the office with Clayburn beside him. The blacksmith was scratching the back of his thick neck.

'I don't get it, Smoke,' he muttered. 'Mebbe I'm not legal minded.'

'Mebbe I'm not either,' Smoke grinned. 'I handed him a line and bolstered it up with a six-gun. That did most of the talking. Anyways, the joint's mine because that agreement says so and the key's the receipt. Better go and see what we've got.'

He turned from the boardwalk to cross the street and then paused as he saw Trixie in the distance leaving Ma Bradshaw's. Immediately he waved his hand in greeting.

'Hey there, Trix, come and join me!' he called.

She paused, glanced in his direction; then as he began to walk towards her she turned abruptly and went the other way. After a moment or two she vanished in the general store, presumably to make some purchases. Smoke came to a stop, frowning.

'If it didn't sound loco I'd say she snubbed me,' he muttered.

'Loco or not,' the blacksmith said, 'she did. Clean a cut as any I ever saw.'

'It doesn't make sense!' Smoke gazed fixedly down the street, half hesitated, and then looked back at Clayburn. 'Must be a mistake somewheres,' he said. 'Mebbe she mistook me for somebody else. I'll deal with it later.'

Though he apparently dismissed the matter from his mind it was plain from his expression that the incident was worrying him. He said no more about it as he accompanied the blacksmith to the great derelict building opposite the Hell's Acres Saloon. Smoke opened the door and then walked into the immense, dusty space, tossing the key up and down in his hand.

As it stood, the building contained nothing but the four walls and a roof with holes in it — but its area was immense. In his mind's eye, as he roamed around slowly, Smoke could already see a bar counter, an office partitioned off from the main space, a rostrum for orchestra and singer — who would be Trixie, of course. There were windows, so grimed they were blotting out the daylight, and rusty fixtures made to contain oil lamps swung in the ceiling.

'Used to be a warehouse,' the blacksmith said. 'I reckon it'll do nicely for your purpose, Smoke.'

'Yeah, I guess so. We'd better get the signboard down.'

They returned outside, removed the sign and tossed it into the building, then re-locked the door.

'Have to call the boys together,' Smoke decided, meditating with his eyes on the busy street. 'I'll see you about it later when I've figgered things out. We'll need timber, fixtures, all kinds of things . . . Okay, thanks for the company. I'd better see what I can do to clean up the sheriff's office: I don't need to keep you from your own work for that.'

Clayburn nodded and went on his way, and Smoke ambled across the street to his office. He nodded to those men and women who greeted him as he passed them; then when he gained his office he had a surprise. A lean, grizzled cow-puncher was standing propping up the door post, evidently waiting for him. At the tie-rack stood his horse, bed-roll and camping equipment at the back of the saddle. Next to it was another loaded horse.

'You th' sheriff around here?' the man asked, then seeing the star on Smoke's shirt he added: 'I ran inter somethin' on the way in. Yuh might be interested.'

'Come right in,' Smoke invited,

opening the door — and in another moment he and the puncher were settled in chairs.

'I've come in frum the north,' the puncher explained, and the dust on his clothes and grime on his face seemed ample evidence of it. 'This is the first town I come to so I thought mebbe I'd better report a body — 'bout eight or ten miles back off the north-ward trail.'

'Body?' Smoke's eyes sharpened.

'Yeah. No ordinary body, neither. It belongs to a marshal. Don't know where frum — no papers or identification uv any kind, but it sure ain't bin there long.'

'How did you find it?' Smoke asked.

'I saw a horse standing by itself off the trail. Struck me as mighty queer for it to be out there, well loaded, and nobody near it — so I investigated. Just near the horse the sand looked disturbed, so I dug down, and found the body. The guy had had his head stoved in, maybe frum a chunk of rock. My guess is that whoever did it didn't use bullets case they could be traced.'

'And where's the body now? And the horse?'

'Horse is outside; I brought it with me. As fur the body I put it back in the sand 'til I could get somebody's help.'

Smoke got quickly to his feet. 'I'll come with you right now. Let's be on our way — What's your name?'

'Hank Bilson. I'm on my way to Oklahoma to join an outfit there.'

Smoke made a note of the name on the scratch pad and then hurried outside. He examined the second horse carefully and found the animal to be a sturdy one, and the equipment untouched. Evidently the marshal had been ready for a long journey.

'I've bin making one or two guesses about this business,' Hank Bilson said, as he swung up to his saddle. 'I get the idea that the marshal was set on and killed, and his horse bolted with fright. Looks like whoever did the attacking couldn't git the horse back — but it returned when all was quiet, as they usually do, and just stood near where his master was buried. Reckon any well-trained cayuse'd do that.'

'Yeah, that's about the size of it,' Smoke admitted, settling on the animal's back. 'Let's see what we can find out.'

They rode swiftly down the street and out of the town by the north end. From then on they went at top speed along the trail, neither of them speaking. In fact Smoke was profoundly worried. The presence of a marshal so near to Hell's Acres spelled only one thing to his mind — danger for Trixie Lee. Whoever had done the killing had certainly performed a service, for the time being. But obviously it could not end up here. The authorities would have to be informed. Another marshal would arrive, this time with an added murder on his agenda. The business was grim — damned grim.

Hank Bilson's guess of about eight miles was fairly accurate. Where the trail branched off from the main route to the mountains and instead expanded into the desert, Bilson drew a halt and pointed. Amidst a few tumbled rocks there was a stretch of churned-up sand. The remaining sand around it was smooth, burning yellow, undisturbed.

'That's it,' Bilson said, and dismounted. Smoke jumped down also and together they moved to the tell-tale spot. It was not long before the loosely-buried form of the dead man was removed.

Smoke tightened his lips as he looked down at the dead young face, the eyes glazed, the head smashed-in by a violent blow. In life, he had obviously been an energetic, virile man. His sand-smothered uniform was enough indication of what his calling had been.

'Nothin' in the pockets,' Bilson said. 'I went through 'em.'

Smoke nodded, then hauled up the body and dragged it to his horse. He put it over the saddle and then turned.

'Better get back into town with this and I'll telegraph the nearest authorities. No idea where this poor devil came from but we'll soon know when I set the wheels moving. I'll have the Hell's Acre coroner hold an inquest and then wait for officials to come over.'

Bilson climbed to his saddle and the journey back began. But neither he nor Smoke returned to town unobserved. Mark Tarlton was in the barber's at the end of a shave and haircut when his casual eye happened to glance through the window. He sat up with a jerk, tearing the towel from about his neck.

'Dad-blamed fool!' he breathed. 'I thought the mug had ditched that stiff deep down — '

'You say something, Mr Tarlton?' the barber asked, coming over with a hot towel.

'No.' Tarlton scrambled up out of his chair. 'Here's your money: never mind the facial.'

He whipped his hat from the peg and darted outside, the surprised eyes of the barber following him. Hurrying along the boardwalk he kept in view the two horsemen, the corpse over the back of

Smoke's mount. Finally he gained the Hell's Acres and sped into the dark interior where his boys were busy tidying up in readiness for business at evening time.

'Hey you mugs!' He summoned them quickly to him. 'A slick job wants doing — right now. You in partic'lar, Seth. Come here!'

The men came across immediately. Seth was a leprous-white being, a cigarette burned to the stub between his lips. He glided rather than moved, and had thin effeminate hands.

'I want a word with you, Seth,' Tarlton told him. 'The rest of you will find a marshal's body stuck on the sheriff's horse outside his office. Get rid of that body! Those are your orders. I don't care what you do, even if you have to kill the tin-badge to do it, but do it! And hurry up!'

The men went immediately, pulling at their guns. Tarlton swung to Seth.

'You're the cause of this, Seth,' he said deliberately. 'Unless that marshal's body is gotten out of the way quick, Smoke Cavendish will have good reason for bringing a horde of law officers into this town — and you know what that means. When I put you on the incoming trail from Denver to watch for any possible marshal I told you to kill him without bullets an' bury him deep. You said you had — Now I find the body on Smoke's horse. How come?'

'I dunno, boss. Just one of these things, I guess.'

'Don't hand me that! You messed up the job and put the lot of us in a spot. I've no time for bunglers, Seth!'

'Mebbe it wus the horse,' Seth said quickly, realizing his life was in danger. 'I couldn't grab that durned cayuse, and I daren't stay monkeyin' around in case somebody came on the trail an' saw me. Mebbe th' horse went back to th' body an' somebody saw it.'

Tarlton breathed hard, his hand on his gun. Then he relaxed. Killing Seth wouldn't do any good. It might rid the world of a rat but it would also dispose of an extremely good gunman. And his death would be too tough to explain — His lips tight, Tarlton swung away and then edged himself beyond the batwings to see how his men were faring.

At the moment they were gathered in an apparently idling, talking group only a few yards from the sheriff's office. Smoke noticed them as he dismounted, but thought nothing of it: idling men were common enough in this sun-blistered waste. He eased the corpse down and let it fall over his shoulder — then it seemed to him that an earthquake had struck him. Hank Bilson, just alighted from his horse, was caught up in the midst of it, too, flattening on his face in the dust beneath a terrific blow to the back of his neck.

Taken unawares by the onslaught, Smoke had little chance to defend himself. Weight of numbers brought him to the ground and a revolver butt on top of the head temporarily blasted the senses out of him. When at length he began to recover he realized that Mark Tarlton was standing nearby, regarding him in grim amusement. Hank Bilson had risen and was rubbing the back of his neck tenderly.

'For a sheriff you're not much good at protecting yourself, Cavendish,' Tarlton remarked.

Smoke got slowly to his feet and looked about him. The horse that had belonged to the marshal — and which he had been using — had gone. There was only Bilson's mount, tied to the rack. In the distance the life of Hell's Acre's main street seemed to be going on undisturbed.

'How much good do you think this is going to do you, Tarlton?' Smoke asked bitterly. 'You've clean given yourself away as being connected with that marshal's corpse. I was just going into my office to make out my report and then telegraph the nearest authorities.'

'I figgered that.' Tarlton gave a shrug.

'Okay, so I've come into the open. I'm admitting that I had that marshal rubbed out, but there isn't anything you can do about it without witnesses.'

'Don't be too sure of that — '

'I am sure of it, otherwise I wouldn't be talking now. And if you call the authorities in from the nearest centre it won't do you any good because they'll want to see the body. You can't produce it, nor the horse. I've taken good care of that. In other words, Cavendish, I've kicked the props from under you. Say what you like to whom you like, but with no proof you're powerless.'

Smoke clenched his fists but he didn't speak. He knew Mark Tarlton was right. Then after a while Smoke asked a question:

'Why did you do it, Tarlton? Not like you to expose your hand so freely.'

'I did it for one very good reason — to protect Trixie. I figger it may have been you who sent for a marshal in the first place. Trixie being so thick with you she's probably told you she's

112

wanted for murder — so naturally the first thing a sheriff will do is throw his weight about and try and get her arrested. You'll not manage it, Cavendish, whilst I'm around.'

'You seem to have forgotten, Tarlton, that Trixie has finished with you, and any 'protection' you can give her.'

'Mebbe she's not so finished with me as you think.'

Both men studied each other for a moment, bristling. Hank Bilson watched them, and waited. Finally Smoke gave a shrug.

'Okay, Tarlton, you've pulled this trick nicely. I'm not going to waste my time looking for a corpse I'll never find — and I won't: you'll have seen to that. I'll let things take care of themselves. There'll be another law officer here pronto to look into things once it's found that that marshal has not reported.'

'Let him come.' Tarlton spread his hands. 'I'm in the clear. Nothing to prove I had anything to do with it. And if you aim to use a law officer to get Trixie railroaded you'll not get far. That needs proof, too, and you haven't got any. I guess from here on the gloves are off. You know who you're fighting — and so do I.'

With that Tarlton turned away and he turned up the boardwalk, leaving Smoke looking after him. Hank Bilson came forward, frowning.

'This means we had all that work fur nothin'?' he demanded. 'That there's nothin' y' can do?'

'That's the size of it,' Smoke answered curtly. 'I should have been more prepared. Things can just stand until another law officer gets into town, as one surely will. You'd better stick around town until that happens; I'll need you as a witness to say you found the body.'

'Okay; I might as well stay here as any place else.'

'Meantime,' Smoke finished, 'I've a private matter to straighten out. Be seeing you around.'

Smoke turned away and hurried across the street to Ma Bradshaw's. Going straight up the stairs he strode along the corridor and knocked lightly on the door of Trixie's room. There was no answer. He frowned, knocked again, then finally turned the knob. Entering, he looked around on the emptiness and at the neatly made bed. The window was slightly open, the curtains wafting in the hot breeze.

Frowning to himself he returned downstairs and looked in the main dining-room. Trixie was not there, either. Finally he sought out Ma Bradshaw herself.

'Trixie?' she repeated, in response to his question. 'I guess she checked out, sheriff.'

'She — what?' Smoke stared blankly. 'But that's utterly impossible, Ma! Why should she?'

'I dunno: she didn't say. I figgered it was kinda funny because I'd sorta gotten it into my head that you an' she wus 'that way' about each other. All

115

she sed was she was goin' to live some place else, but didn't say where. Then she paid up and went.'

'And left no word for me, or anything?'

''fraid not.'

The memory of Trixie's behaviour in the main street returned to Smoke as he stood thinking. Finally he wandered out of the kitchen regions and to the outdoors again, after which he started on a search which occupied him until well into the afternoon. He finished up in his sheriff's office, grim and disconsolate. He had tried every possible place where Trixie might have lodged, and discovered no sign of her. The only solution seemed to be that she had blown town entirely.

'Reckon that's about it,' Smoke muttered. 'Tarlton probably gave her the tip-off about a marshal being in the region and she took fright. She might be just any place.'

Actually, the girl was not 'any place'. At that moment she was at Tarlton's

116

ranch, two miles out of town, whither she had gone after careful consideration. Rather than meet Smoke and be forced to ignore him, or tie herself up in difficult explanations, she had decided to seek Tarlton's protection again, for what it was worth. He was the only possible person who could save her from the law, and it was worth tolerating him if only for that. Had Trixie stayed in town a little while longer after making her purchases in the general store she would have seen the fracas outside the sheriff's office and perhaps have straightened herself out — but at that time she had been right out of town and still under the impression that Smoke was a marshal bent on her arrest.

Evening would be the problem for Trixie, when she returned to the saloon — but then she would have Tarlton to help her and she little doubted but that he would be able to keep Smoke in his place.

Smoke, for his part, debated the

wisdom of tackling Tarlton direct and demanding to know where Trixie was — then he abandoned the idea as he realized that Tarlton would never break down.

'And I can't spend my time roaming around looking for her,' Smoke growled, studying the grimy office. 'If I left here and did that I'd spoil everything I've planned out. Only answer to that one is to get on with my own plans and mebbe Trixie will return one day — or mebbe I'll get news of her.'

Decided, he got to his feet, set out a belated lunch from the provisions he had brought in with him, and then afterwards went in search of Clayburn.

'I want all the boys at a meeting tonight,' Smoke said. 'In that building I've bought. We've got to decide what we need and how we can get it. Let them know to be there around eight.'

'Okay,' Clayburn agreed promptly.

And further up the street Tarlton was seated in Luke Bairstow's office, eyeing the lawyer with a snakelike stare.

'I keep you well paid an' comfortable, Bairstow, for what?' Tarlton demanded. 'So you can double-cross me on the first occasion.'

'No question of a double-cross when a gun's pointing at you,' Bairstow retorted, trying to defend himself. 'Cavendish had all the aces in his hand: I had to sell or get a bullet through me.'

'You may get one anyways before I'm finished with you,' Tarlton snapped; then he fell to thought. 'Not that it really matters,' he went on, his tone more conciliatory. 'I knew Cavendish was going to buy that joint of mine to turn it into a rival saloon.'

'If you knew and didn't want to sell why didn't you stop me?' Bairstow demanded.

'Because I did want you to sell, you lug! The thing I object to is you selling without asking for my say-so. Anyways, skip it. I'll see that Cavendish never gets his saloon built even if I have to kill him first. All we've got to do is to let him think he's doing nicely. He's paid, and the transfer of property is signed — Okay, let it stay that way. But if you ever hand out any more of my property like that without so much as a by-your-leave, I'll get another lawyer. In fact I'll have to because you won't be around.'

With that Tarlton left the office and headed for his saloon. He found his men making the final touches to the place ready for the evening opening. They glanced up from their various jobs as he came amongst them.

'Ditch that body and the horse?' he questioned.

'Sure thing, boss,' one of them grinned. 'Right off the desert trail where nobody c'never find anythin'. Pity we had ter shoot th' cayuse too: a good animal. But no other way. We buried it near the stiff. Nothin' to worry about. Nobody'll ever find anythin'.'

'They'd better not,' Tarlton growled; then as he came into the midst of the men he continued: 'From here on you've all got to keep on the watch.

This sheriff of ours might try just anything, and we've got to be prepared. Whenever any of you see him and some of his pardners gathering for a meeting find out all you can about it so's I can know in advance. I don't have to tell you how to get information — especially you, Seth.'

The leprous Seth gave his slant grin and lowered a thin hand to his gun.

'Cavendish may also try and make trouble where Trixie Lee is concerned,' Tarlton added. 'If he does, do what you like with him but show him he isn't welcome. Got it?'

The men nodded promptly and glanced significantly at each other.

'Then that's all for now,' Tarlton said. 'I'm going home to get ready for evening — an' to let Trixie know I'm more than glad to have her back,' he added with a grin; then the batwings swung back and forth he passed out to the boardwalk.

5

At eight o'clock prompt Smoke was presiding over his meeting of stalwarts. He had with him a list of requirements which he had prepared, in which was included an itinerary of the various fixtures and building materials needed to bring the shell of a building up to date.

'None of you are working partners in this,' he said, when he had read out the list and had it approved, 'but since you have decided to help me of your own free will, even to assisting in the rebuilding and the fitting up of the various necessities, I'm going to see to it that you all get a percentage of the profits when the saloon starts paying off. It may take some months, but we'll succeed or else.'

'Where's the timber coming from, sheriff?' one man asked.

'Dodge City. I've already contacted a firm there by telegraph and they'll be sending the first timber consignment tomorrow. We'll pick it up at the station here. That's the main thing we need — timber. We want it for the new roofing, for making the bar, the partitions, the tables — everything. If we can't work with the raw materials we're not the men I think we are. I reckon there must be some good carpenters amongst you.'

'Three,' said the blacksmith. 'And all the ironwork we need I'll do — willingly. Ever think what you're going to call this place, Smoke?'

'Yeah . . . I did. The 'Trixie Lee'.' And Smoke gave a grim smile.

'Trixie'll like that,' one of the men grinned.

'I'm hoping so. I'm hoping it'll bring her back into town, too. I reckon she's walked out, for no reason that I can rightly figger.'

'Walked out?' Clayburn repeated, surprised. 'Last I saw of her she was heading out of town to the south, but she wasn't loaded as though she figgered on goin' any long distance. She'd got enough stuff for mebbe a change of clothes, but that's all. No bed-roll, no provisions.'

Smoke's expression changed. 'When was this?'

'Not long after I left you this morning. I was in my livery stable and saw her ride past. I was goin' to ask her if she'd really cut you when we saw her in the street, only she was gone too fast.'

'So she was headed south, but not for a long journey,' Smoke mused. 'Wonder where she was going?'

'Only one place I can think of,' the blacksmith replied. 'The Double-J spread. That's Tarlton's place, two miles out of town. Wouldn't be anywhere else that Trixie would be interested in, I imagine.'

Smoke clenched his fist. 'Why the heck didn't I think of that before?' he muttered. 'The way I'm looking at it it seems that for some reason she — ' He stopped, remembering that her possible reason for departure was because of the presence of a marshal near town.

'I'm riding out there this minute,' he decided. 'You know how things are here, fellas. I'll contact you when the timber's arrived and we'll get busy.'

He hurried outside, all thought of his plans for the saloon forgotten for the moment at the realization that Trixie was possibly near at hand all the time. Taking his horse — which he had bought from Clayburn only two hours before — from the tie-rack outside his sheriff's office he mounted it and sped away down the trail in the evening light. It seemed to him as good an opportunity as there ever would be to catch Trixie alone since, at this hour, Tarlton himself would be in the saloon. The girl herself would surely not be there — as far as Smoke could see — in case the law happened to catch up.

Or would she? Smoke began to slow up as doubt assailed him. Finally he brought his horse to a halt entirely and looked back over his shoulder. He was nearer to Hell's Acres Saloon than the Double-J spread at the moment, so perhaps before he went any further he might —

He swung his horse around and began to head back. And at this time Clayburn, the blacksmith, was in a spot of trouble. With a six-gun in his spine he was being marched round the back of the buildings, at the mercy of Seth and two hard-bitten gunmen. He had come out ahead of the other boys in the ancient building and, consequently, had been the first to be nailed by the watchful Seth and his fellow coyotes. Right now Clayburn was on his way to the back entrance of the Hell's Acres Saloon — and within ten minutes he finished up in a rear room and found himself securely tied to a chair.

'I wonder,' Seth mused, with a glance at his colleagues, 'if this guy is as good at talkin' about other things as he is at preachin' sermons.'

'Talking about what?' Clayburn demanded, straining his powerful muscles in an endeavour to break free — and failing.

'In case yuh don't know it, feller, war's bin declared in this town,' Seth explained, with his crooked smile. 'Between the boss and the sheriff. No punches pulled. Naterally, the boss wants to know just what goes on in the enemy camp — and you can tell us. What've yuh been meetin' tonight fur? What's coming up?'

Clayburn did not answer. His jaw set stolidly and he gave Seth a defiant glare. Seth's grin widened, then suddenly his hand slapped violently back and forth across Clayburn's rugged face. The blows stung viciously but they did not bring forth any murmur.

'Okay,' Seth said, shrugging. 'The boss said go the limit to find out information, so we may as well.'

He turned aside and picked up a coil of wire, its ends linked by a piece of tough wood. Slipping the wire over the

127

blacksmith's forehead Seth tightened it until it had a firm grip. Then his low, slurred voice began talking again.

'Ever seen cheese cut with a wire, Clayburn? Slices right through it — clean as a whistle. You think yuh tougher than a cheese?'

Clayburn still did not say anything, but sweat started on his rough-hewn features.

'Just the simplest thing I'm asking,' Seth said gently, his hand closing on the stick in the wire-ends. 'Just tell me what you and that no-account sheriff talked about.'

When silence greeted him Seth's face became even whiter than usual and his fingers tightened the wire viciously by turning the stick. A trickle of blood began to course down the blacksmith-parson's face as the skin was cut. The two other men glanced at each other. They had not the cold, inhuman brutality of Seth who was recognized to be the most vindictive killer who had ever come to Hell's Acres.

The wire tightened again and Clayburn gasped. He knew full well that if he didn't speak the merciless wire would cut through his skull by degrees — and the thought of that was more than he could take.

'Okay!' he gasped. 'Hold it! I'll tell you . . .'

'I'll believe that when yuh start talkin',' Seth retorted, his mouth hard. 'Git on with it . . .'

He gave the wire another vicious turn just for luck and Clayburn could not help himself screaming under the blinding pressure.

'We — we talked about fixtures!' he cried, shouting under the promptings of pain.

'Fixtures? What sorta fixtures?'

'A bar, mirrors, gaming tables, chairs — the whole works for a saloon —'

'Keep talkin'!' Seth snapped.

'That's all there is, I guess —'

'No it ain't, fella. Where's all the timber coming frum?'

'Dodge City.'

'When?'

'Tomorrow,' Clayburn gasped out. 'For heaven's sake get this wire from me . . .'

Seth reflected, then with a shrug he unscrewed the loop and hung the wire on one side. Clayburn sagged in his ropes, blood trickling down his face from the deep cut ringing his forehead and passing over his ears.

'Untie him,' Seth ordered, and his men looked surprised.

'That such a good idea, Seth?' one of them asked. 'If he goes back an' tells Smoke everythin' where's our chance of springing a surprise — ?'

'I said untie him!' Seth snarled. 'Do as yuh damned well told!'

He was obeyed and, bleeding and dazed, Clayburn was hauled up. Seth pinned him with a hand in his shirt front.

'Listen, fella, if yore as good at prayers fur yuhself as y'are fur everybody else, yuh'd better say some. I'm goin' t'blast th' livin' daylights outa yuh. No other way uv makin' yuh keep quiet about what's happened here.'

Clayburn stared at the dead-white face with its slanting smile.

'You — you mean you'd shoot me down, when I'm undefended and can't — '

'Yeah, that's what I mean. Like this!'

Seth's gun exploded twice. He stood watching the blacksmith's big figure tumble sharply. It was Trixie who stood on the threshold, dressed in her sequined gown, an expression of fixed horror on her face. Slowly her eyes moved from the sprawled Clayburn to Seth. He put his gun back in its holster and impaled her with his cruel eyes.

'Well, what d'yuh want?' he demanded.

'I — I heard everything he — he said — ' Trixie glanced again at the motionless figure. 'You were torturing him, weren't you?'

'Any business of yours?' Seth's eyes didn't move from her.

'When I heard the shot I came to see what had happened. My dressing room's next door, remember, and the partition's only thin. You're planning something against Smoke, aren't you?'

'Mebbe. Mebbe not. If yore wise yuh'll get outa here — and quick! And don't forget which way t'go, neither. If yuh run to the sheriff yuh'll run inter the law as well — so best go to the boss and forget what yuh saw here.'

Trixie hesitated then half turned at the sound of footsteps in the corridor. It was Tarlton who came into the room and stood looking at the corpse for a moment.

'I heard the shots,' he said briefly. 'Next time if you have to take care of a guy don't make so much noise about it. It attracts attention . . . I suppose it was necessary to rub out this first deputy, or did you just get trigger-happy?'

'Didn't want him t'go back ter Smoke and tell everythin' did yuh?' Seth demanded.

'This is deliberate murder, Mark,' Trixie said, turning her angry eyes to him. 'First Seth here tortured Clayburn and then shot him dead. I don't know why you tolerate such a filthy killer around the place — '

Seth took a step forward, his face livid and his fist clenched. Then he stopped before the look in Tarlton's eye.

'Take it easy, Seth,' he warned deliberately. 'Trixie is my responsibility. One wrong move out of you and I'll kick your face in. Now, what happened about Clayburn here? What did he have to tell?'

Seth gave the details, his voice and face sullen.

'Okay, that's news worth having,' Tarlton mused. 'You boys make arrangements to stop that timber consignment getting in tomorrow. I don't care what you do — even if you chuck the timber into one of the chasms as the train cuts through the mountains near Jetmore, but get rid of it. I guess there's only one train headed to this dump from Dodge City and that gets in around three in the afternoon. See you intercept it at Jetmore and do your job properly.'

'I'll fix it,' Seth promised, glancing at his men.

Tarlton nodded. 'You'd better. Now get this stiff out the way he came in, and make sure you bury him good and deep. We'll have Smoke around looking for trouble before long, but if he only suspects and can't prove we're in the clear . . . Come on, Trixie, time you got back and gave the customers a song.'

He caught her arm and held on to it as they went down the narrow corridor.

'Naturally you'll keep what you know to yourself,' he said briefly. 'Blabbing anything to that law officer will do you no good, and you know it . . . now get into the saloon and start singing. I've got to finish in my office.'

Trixie received a final shove which made her stumble. Her face bitter she entered the smoky saloon and then made for the rostrum. Half way there she paused and looked about her in alarm. She had just caught sight of Smoke arriving at the bar.

'Where's Tarlton?' Smoke demanded

of the bar-keep, as he picked up his glass of rye.

'Don't know, sheriff. He went out back someplace.'

'Trixie still here?' Smoke looked about him.

'Sure thing. She's about due to give a song. Last I saw of her she'd headed for her dressing room — '

'All right, I see her,' Smoke interrupted, putting down his glass quickly — and he made his way swiftly between the tables. Just as Trixie was about to bob out of sight down the corridor again he caught her arm and whirled her to him.

'Just a minute, Trix — What's the idea?'

She tried to draw free but the compulsion of his arm would not allow her. His blue eyes were fixed on her more in puzzled hurt than anything else.

'I — I got the idea we couldn't make out,' she said lamely. 'Now let me go, Smoke; I've a number to do.'

'Not 'til you've explained why you walked out on me without a word. What did I do, anyways? I thought we'd fixed everything up and that everything was plain sailing.'

'I had to move,' she said desperately. 'I can't explain it, Smoke. Please — let me go!'

'Did you get on the move because of a marshal, perhaps?'

She looked at him, wide-eyed. 'Yes,' she whispered. 'I guess that was the — '

'Let the lady go, fella,' snapped the voice of Seth from further down the corridor. 'Yuh sheriff's duties don't include maulin' the boss's womenfolk.'

Smoke spun round, and unconsciously released his hold. Trixie took advantage of it and hurried away. Undecided, Smoke looked first one way and then the other.

'Better beat it, sheriff,' Seth suggested. 'By this back door here. Yuh not gettin' a chance t'follow Trixie. Can't yuh see she doesn't want yuh? Come on — move.'

Smoke began advancing slowly, keeping his hands raised. Seth reached out and closed the door of the room from which he had emerged. Smoke vaguely wondered why, and kept on going as Seth indicated a doorway at the end of the corridor which led out to the open.

'Think yuhself lucky I don't take yuh gun frum yuh, or else drill yuh,' Seth remarked. 'I would only I got orders frum the boss. It don't pay ter rub out the sheriff: better he meets with an accident.'

Smoke had come opposite the door when he heard words from inside the room beyond.

' . . . reckon this'll be one first deputy the sheriff'll be wonderin' about fur a long time to come. Grab his feet.'

Smoke stopped. Seth's eyes slitted and his gun came up more sharply. Smoke could smell mystery and maybe murder in the air and for a moment forgot everything else. His right fist crashed out straight into the face of the gunhawk and slammed him hard against the doorpost. He tried to get his gun straight again but the fist crashed under his jaw. This time he hit the door itself and his weight snapped it open on its catch and pitched him into the room beyond. The two gunhawks holding Clayburn's dead body between them and just on their way out looked around in surprise.

'Drop it!' Smoke spat, as Seth's hand moved for his fallen gun.

Instead, Seth kicked out his right boot and the heavy toe caught Smoke a resounding crack on the shin. He gasped, his gun shifting position, then the two men holding Clayburn had dropped him and plunged on Smoke instead.

The man on his left he sent sprawling with a terrific uppercut. The other man he seized round the waist, swung him off his feet, then brought him crashing down with a sledgehammer blow on the back of his neck.

Seth half rose and aimed his gun, only to flatten out again as Smoke plunged on top of him, wrenched his arm, and whirled the gun out of his grip. With his weapon gone the gunman was yellow right through. It showed in his pale venomous eyes as he was swung to his feet.

'So you killed Clayburn, huh?' Smoke asked, his eyes aflame with fury. 'And from the look of his forehead yuh tortured him first — Okay, fella, I don't like friends treated that way. I'm no killer but by hell you're going to settle part of the account until I can legally fix you for a necktie party.'

A ball of fire burst behind Seth's eyes as Smoke's iron fist struck him with stupefying impact on the nose. He hit the wall and partly rebounded, to find his head snapped before a killing punch on the ear. Half numbed he made an effort to hit back and Smoke grunted at a body blow. Almost immediately he recovered and swung up his left, sending the gunhawk tottering until he hit the table. He grasped it fiercely and tried to swing it round, then he found his breath exploded from him as a sledgehammer imbedded itself in his stomach. Choking and gulping, his hands clawing at his middle, he reeled about the room — to meet a blow under the chin that made him straight as a poker for a moment. Blood crimsoned his mouth as unintentionally his teeth had snapped shut over the end of his tongue.

Black shapes danced in front of him, then they took on whirling edges as pain hit him again on his damaged nose. Without breath, his arms flailing, he absorbed blow after blow, his face purpling — then his senses blasted out of him in a roar of sound as the side of his jaw cracked under the deadly knuckles. He lifted from his feet, spun backwards over the table, and hit the thin partition wall with such force that it splintered, flinging his head and shoulders through it. He lay motionless, legs twitching with reaction.

Slowly Smoke straightened, scooping back dishevelled hair from his face. He looked down at the other two gunmen who were slowly recovering, then turned quickly — until a voice in the doorway stopped him.

'You can leave your deputy right where he is, Cavendish.'

Tarlton came into the room, his gun at the ready. He looked at his gunhawks contemptuously as they staggered up, then his expression changed as Seth failed to rise. Motioning the two dazed men to keep Smoke covered he stooped and dragged Seth up from the shattered wall. Immediately he began to slide down again, crumpling up.

'Nice work,' Tarlton commented acidly. 'You broke his neck, sheriff.'

'Which evens the score a bit,' Smoke retorted, breathing hard. 'You killed my first deputy; I killed your best gunman. Anything else?'

'I could probably organize a necktie party and make you swing for Seth's murder.'

'It was an accident — and you'd better not try any necktie parties with me, Tarlton. The people aren't too much in favour of you after your wheel-fixing. You're lucky you can do any business at all — and I guess you won't when I've opened my own place.'

'If you live that long,' Tarlton commented.

There was silence. Smoke looked at the guns trained on him. He was outnumbered three to one, and was no fool.

'Seth's my repayment for the time being, Tarlton,' he said briefly. 'I can't pin the murder of Clayburn on you because I didn't see who did it — but I figger it was Seth at your orders. He's been repaid for that. Later I'll come round to you and fix you — for good.'

Tarlton said nothing. Smoke picked up his fallen hat and put it on, then without another word, even though he was half expecting a gun to be fired in his back, he left the room. In a moment or two he had reached the saloon, to find Trixie on the rostrum struggling with a song. Beauty and figure she might have — in fact did have — but she certainly could not sing. Smoke gave a rather helpless smile as he looked at her. She saw him, but took no notice. Frowning, he moved to a nearby table and sat down. Ultimately she would be bound to come down from that rostrum, and then —

But Smoke did not find things that easy. He had hardly settled at the table and refreshed himself with rye before the corpulent figure of Carmichael sat down opposite him. His pink face was smiling as urbanely as usual.

'Checking up on law and order, Smoke?' he enquired.

'Yeah — sure.' Smoke did not want to be bothered. He had his eyes fixed on the white-skinned girl in the sequinned gown.

'Haven't seen you knocking about much. I'm planning to take Tarlton for another ride tonight. Guess it's time I did — and I can do with more money. Tomorrow I'll try again and then again. Don't always hit a winning streak, you know, but once I do — '

''Scuse me,' Smoke interrupted, rising. 'I've got to dash. I want a word with Trixie — See you again, and I'm still grateful for that money you loaned me.'

'That's what I wanted to ask you about. How's about that building? Did you — '

'You and me have unfinished business, Trix,' he said quietly. 'We were just talking about a marshal when we were interrupted.'

She gave an anxious glance around her, then as the only retreat was into the saloon where Smoke could follow her she stood her ground.

'Do you suppose there's anything you can do about that?' she asked bitterly. 'Stop playing with me, Smoke! Either ignore me entirely or arrest me, but don't keep talking in insinuations.'

Smoke looked puzzled. 'I don't get it, Trix. What possible reason could I have for wanting to arrest you? It doesn't make sense. You — '

'You're on my property, sheriff, and as long as you are not here on official business I've the right to order you off. And I'm doing it. Get out!'

Smoke and Trixie both stood looking at Tarlton as he came slowly towards them from the passage. There was cold menace in his dark eyes as he put his arm about the girl's shoulders.

'This the way you want it, Trix?' Smoke asked quietly.

'I — I guess so,' she faltered.

'Then I don't understand it. Mebbe I'll never figger out women. The way I looked at it you'd thrown this chiseller overboard.'

'I don't like your language, Cavendish,' Tarlton snapped. 'Get out — and quick!'

Smoke hesitated, his blue eyes on Trixie's face. He found it impossible to analyse her expression, so finally he turned and left. Trixie watched him go across the saloon, then she relaxed a little as the batwings swung back and forth after his departure.

'This sort of thing can't go on much longer, Mark,' she said seriously. 'Either I've got to let Smoke arrest me, or else he's got to be run out of town — and you certainly won't manage that. He's too tough for you.'

'Is he?' Tarlton gave a sour grin. 'We'll see! Anyways, he's out of the way for the moment so just make yourself comfortable. I'll join you later and we can go back to my place together. Stick by me, Trix, and you've nothing to fear.'

Trixie watched him depart across the saloon, presumably to catch up on neglected conversation with his customers. Moodily she considered what she ought to do next. She had to change, of course, and then wait until the saloon closed and go home with Tarlton. She didn't fear going home with him: he was tough but never offensive, about the only thing in his favour. Then, suddenly, she heard the tail end of a conversation:

' . . . his cayuse wus just standin' there. Well trained, I reckon. Come right back t'where his boss wus, even if he wus dead. One thing about a marshal's horse — usually well trained. Yes, sir!'

Trixie turned slowly as the conversation registered on her mind. It was the word 'marshal' which had caught her attention. After a moment she caught sight of a whiskery saddle-tramp seated at a nearby table. He was obviously the worse for liquor. With him was a thin nosed cattle dealer who evidently liked idle gossip.

'And you mean you just let that marshal's body lie there an' rot?' the cattle dealer asked, in surprise. 'Seems to me you should have reported it.'

''Course I reported it!' Hank Bilson glared belligerently. 'I told th' sheriff and we dug the body out. Then what happened? The body was frisked away afore we could do anythin'. Where it is now I'll be durned if I — hup! 'scuse me — know.'

Trixie moved abruptly, catching hold of the saddle-tramp's shoulder. He looked up in surprise and then grinned.

'Hello, kid! Nicest thing I've seen so fur around this two-cent joint. How's about a drink? C'mon — sit down.'

His hand went round her waist compellingly and tried to drag her forward. She was equal to it. Holding the table stopped her movement towards his knee.

'What's this about a marshal?' she asked, and then glanced around her to be sure Tarlton was some distance away.

'A marshal? Aw, who th' heck cares, anyways? Lots more interestin' things ter talk about. C'mon, sit down!'

This time Trixie could not save herself. She landed on Hank's knee with a thump and was held there tightly.

'That's better,' he grinned. 'Nice an' friendly. Now about that drink — '

'Brandy,' Trixie said, smiling, realizing she had to sell herself for the moment to learn what she wanted.

The waiter came over and looked at Trixie in surprise, knowing that she was neither sexy nor a drinker of hard liquor. Just the same he had the order and fulfilled it. Trixie picked up the glass of brandy, managed to tip some out and then gave the impression of having drank it.

'Now, what about this marshal?' she asked tensely. 'I want to know about him.'

'Why? Friend uv yours?'

'Could be. Tell me . . . '

'Worth a kiss, ain't it? Infurmation's usually paid fur around these parts. I don't want money, so I reckon a kiss is th' only other thing.'

Trixie gave a look at the cattle dealer, but he evidently had no intention of interfering. He sat watching, a sly grin on his thin features. Then before Trixie could decide what to do she found herself tugged backwards fiercely and the saddle-tramp planted his lips on her cheek.

'That's better,' he grinned, as she straightened again and tried to control her fury. 'As fur that marshal he ain't uv much interest t'you or anybody else. He's dead, I reckon.'

'How long had he been dead when you found him?'

'No more than a few hours, I guess.'

'Find out his name?'

'Nope. I — Say, what is this?' Hank Bilson looked at her intently, his arm tightening about her waist. 'I thought you an' me wus goin' ter get friendly. That's what yuh paid fur, isn't it? T'be nice to the customers?'

'Sure — sure,' Trixie agreed, trying to smile and finding Hank's bony leg by no means a comfortable seat. 'But this marshal interests me. Where was he from?'

'I dunno. There weren't no signs. Somebody had frisked the guy afore the sheriff an' me got t'him. Nothing but his uniform — no badge, no nothin' . . . '

With a sudden hard effort Trixie dragged herself free of the imprisoning arm and stood up. Bilson looked at her in annoyance.

'Now what?' he demanded. 'When d'you an' me start to get really friendly? I'm not a hard guy to please.'

Trixie backed away, her face pale and her eyes wide, and into the back corridor. She had time to notice that Tarlton, busy talking at the distant bar, had not noticed what had transpired. There remained the possibility, of course, that Hank Bilson would pursue her. Half intoxicated as he was he might do just anything — and he did.

She had just reached her dressing-room and was closing the door when Bilson's foot jammed between it and the frame. In one powerful heave he slammed it back and stood glaring at her in the light of the oil lamps. His face was greasy with sweat, his mouth tight.

'Thought yuh'd give me the brush off, huh?' he demanded, lurching inwards. 'No dame does that ter me — not when I like her like I do you. Yuh've got what it takes, kid . . . '

Trixie backed away, her face pale and

her eyes wide. She had never felt so alone in her life. Tarlton was far away at the bar and Smoke was — well, anywhere. She came up against the dressing-table with a sudden bump. Bilson circled so that he faced her, his hands opening and shutting.

Then suddenly he leapt, and Trixie was unprepared for it. In one savage movement he seized the front of her dress and ripped with all his strength. Sequins descended in a cloud to the floor and, bereft of support from the shoulder straps the dress slipped down.

Trixie made a frantic effort to dodge, but Bilson, inflamed with drink, was not to be balked. Seizing her arms tightly he bore her down on the sofa, then pinning her with one hand he ripped away the remains of her dress — Trixie's hands lashed out and left deep, bleeding gouge marks down his face. For answer he tore off her shoes, then her stockings, but so intent was he on the job he forgot Trixie had her hands free. She squirmed savagely and caught hold of the oil lamp on the table beside her. Swinging it in an arc she brought the heavy base down on the top of Bilson's skull. He groaned and slipped down to the floor amidst a cascade of spluttering oil-flames.

Instantly Trixie was on her feet, batting frantically at herself as the flames leapt upon her flimsy clothing. She whirled round and snatched her gown from the door, hugging it tight and smothering herself in a cloud of smoke. Half choked, she staggered out into the passage-way, leaving behind her a leaping column of flame which was seizing on clothes and dry wood with tremendous avidity.

Her arrival in the saloon, bare-footed, hair streaming, face dirty, and wrapped in the gown, brought stares of amazement. Immediately Tarlton hurried over to her.

'Trix, what on earth — '

'The place is on fire,' she panted. 'My dressing-room. A saddle-tramp got fresh and — and knocked over the oil lamp. If you don't want the place burned to ashes get busy quick.'

Tarlton swung, motioned to several of his boys, and then hurtled out to the back regions. Since Trixie's words had not carried very far none of the customers was aware of what was really happening so no panic ensued. Then Trixie became aware of the odd figure she was cutting and in sudden embarrassment she turned and made for Tarlton's private room. She knew there was a dress there — one special one she wore at times to 'suit his mood'. There was also a pair of shoes to match it.

She found both in their usual place and hurried into them, then she straightened her hair and cleaned the dirt from her face. This done she opened the door and went along the corridor to take another look at the saloon. Evidently the fire was being brought under control for there was no sign of it having spread to the pool room itself.

Right now, Trixie's main idea was to

get out before Tarlton came back. She had learned enough to realize that she had been completely double-crossed . . . so she hurried to the window, opened it, and slid on to the low built verandah. In a slithering rush she went down it and landed with a bump in the dust of the main street. She gave a glance at the saloon, to see smoke gushing from the back regions — but very little flame — then she hurried across the street to Ma Bradshaw's. Thankfully she shut the front door behind her and stood for a moment regaining her breath.

Ma Bradshaw, hearing the door slam, peered out of the kitchen regions, and then gave a start of surprise as she beheld Trixie. Certainly Trixie looked odd. Her hair was awry after her slide down the roof, yet her dress was of the most exquisite design. She had no stockings, but the latest style in shoes. She was half well-dressed and half a trollop.

'Trixie!' Ma came hurrying forward,

her fat quivering, 'I thought you'd checked out — '

'Maybe I have — maybe not.' Trixie put a hand to her forehead worriedly. 'I hardly know what I am doing at the moment. Where's Smoke? Is he in?'

'Sure thing — in his room. Came in ten minutes ago — '

Trixie did not hesitate any longer. She raced up the staircase and to Smoke's room. He opened the door as she knocked and then started back, half in anger.

'Contrary girl, aren't you?' he asked shortly, closing the door behind her. 'Now what? Last I saw of you you'd definitely signed yourself over to Tarlton — '

'Smoke, I've found out the truth.' Trixie caught at his arm tightly. 'You're not a marshal after all.'

'Huh?' Smoke stared at her. 'Me? A marshal? What in heck gave you that idea?'

'Mark told me you were Grant Caldwell, a Denver City law officer, making a play for me to get all the information you could before arresting me for . . . for that murder.'

Smoke was silent for a moment, trying to sort out the bewildering statement. Then, frowning, he motioned the girl to a chair.

'Tell me more,' he invited, perched on the table edge.

Trixie did so, giving every detail. She finished in a rush of words.

'The moment I'd figured everything out from that saddle-tramp I realized how completely Mark had double-crossed me. Obviously he did it to keep me away from you . . . So I decided to come over right away. It wasn't easy, since that saddle-tramp followed me up. In getting away from him I set fire to my dressing-room. Maybe the fire's quelled now . . . '

She got up and went to the window, gazing intently across the street. The flare of lights from the Hell's Acres was there as usual but no sign of flames. Evidently Tarlton and his boys had caught the conflagration in time. Then at the grasp of Smoke's powerful hands on her shoulders Trixie turned.

'You've one trouble you'll have to outgrow, Trix,' he said, smiling. 'You're too easily led — especially, by a two-timer like Tarlton . . . What has me worried is: what happens now? If he knows you've come here — '

'He doesn't. He's too busy with the fire. He mustn't know I've come — ever. He'd probably kill me — especially as I came also to warn you.'

'Warn me? Concerning what?'

'You've a consignment of timber coming in tomorrow from Dodge City, haven't you? Well, I was there when Mark made arrangements with Seth and his boys to ditch your timber at Jetmore, near the pass. You'll have to stop them.'

'Mmmm.' Smoke's eyes narrowed. 'Thanks for the tip-off, Trix. It won't be Seth who'll do that job: he's been taken care of. Some of the other boys, I suppose. Anyway, I'll look after it — All that apart, what are you going to do? You can't keep dodging between Tarlton and me. Sooner or later he'll catch you out, and then — '

'So far he doesn't know I've learned the truth,' Trixie broke in. 'I can make an excuse for vanishing tonight: tell him I was afraid of the fire, or something. The point is this — if I stay beside him I can probably get to know when he's planning something against you, and so I can give you warning.'

'Yes, but it's a risk I don't like you taking, Trix. I guess it might be better for you to stay right beside me.'

She shook her blonde head. 'That way we'd never know what was coming next. I'll take my chance . . . ' She broke off and thought for a moment. 'Even though I've found out that you are not a marshal I'm still worried. What do you suppose that marshal was after? Me?'

'How can I say? Might have been just coincidence. We've no guarantee that he was coming to Hell's Acres, even if we do know from the badge you saw that he belonged to the Denver City authorities. Only thing to do, Trix, is try and forget it.'

'And you haven't reported the murder to Denver City?'

'No.' Smoke's face became grim. 'No point in my doing so with the body gone. I can't prove what I'm saying, and just my word for it along with that of a saddle-tramp like Bilson won't be any use. Evidently it was Bilson who attacked you, and had I been around I'd have torn him wide open.'

'And lost yourself a valuable witness if you ever need him for when the law does catch up . . . ' Trixie sighed. 'Well, I'd better be getting back before Mark finds my disappearance too obvious. We'll be closing soon, then I'll have to go back to his ranch with him.'

'You could stay here in your old room and tell him you've changed your mind.'

'No; I'm going through with this. Unofficial spy. You don't have to worry.

I know Mark and though I don't like him in the usual way I can trust him to keep to himself. I'm not alone with him at his spread, you know. There is a woman who looks after the domestic part, as well as an Indian squaw, and a general man.'

'Well, I still don't like it — but good luck just the same. I'll keep my eye on you as best I can, and I'll take care that my timber isn't ditched, too.'

Smoke moved to the door and held it open. He stooped to kiss the girl and then held her for a moment.

'Next time don't get led up the garden,' he reproved her.

'Cross my heart, Smoke!' She gave a serious smile; then she turned and went down the corridor.

6

She found upon arriving back at the Hell's Acres that most of the customers had departed for the night. Gambling, too, was over for this session — and to judge from the look on the face of fat Carmichael, having a final drink, he had not done too well. Not that Trixie was interested in him: her eyes moved instead to Tarlton as he stood propped up on his elbows at the bar watching her approach.

'What happened to you?' he asked briefly, pondering her dress and shoes. 'I've been hunting all over for you.'

'Sorry, Mark. I guess I panicked when the fire broke out. I was scared of it involving the whole saloon, so I cleared out quickly. When I saw things were not so bad I decided I might as well venture back.'

'What gave you the notion to leave by

the window?' Tarlton asked. 'I found it open in my private room — and that dress and your shoes gone.'

'I had to put something on, didn't I?' Trixie looked at him under her eyes, half frightened by his tone. 'As for my going by the window I wanted to get out, but quick . . . How did you make out with the fire?'

'Killed it.' Tarlton finished his last drink and plonked down the empty glass on the counter. 'Not much damage done, though all your dresses have gone up in smoke. The biggest damage was to that saddle-tramp who attacked you. He was dead.'

Trixie gave a start. 'Dead? But how could he be?'

'His body was severely burned for one thing, and for another his skull was cracked. I don't quite figger how it got that way since he was lying on the floor well away from any heavy furniture. I suppose,' Tarlton added, his voice at the same dead-level pitch, 'you didn't slug him with the oil lamp and so start the fire? That could have cracked his skull, if the base of the lamp had struck him edgewise.'

'Yes — I hit him,' Trixie admitted. 'I didn't say so at first in case everything went up in flames: if it had you'd have blamed me for it. As it is, with only negligible damage, I can give you the facts. That saddle-tramp had me pinned down on the sofa. He was drunk and had only one idea in his mind — So I let him have it. That's self-defence; just in case you're thinking I've added another 'murder' to my record.'

'I wasn't thinking anything of the sort. You had to protect yourself, sure — same as you did from that guy in Denver. I guess he deserved all he got. I should report it to the sheriff, only I don't aim to. That saddle-tramp had nobody likely to miss him and the less said about his death the better. I've had the boys ditch him — Meantime,' Tarlton finished, 'there's something I want to ask you. Come along to my office; it's quieter.'

Trixie followed him, vaguely wondering what was coming. There was something in Mark Tarlton's attitude which she could not quite understand, and it made her heart beat much too painfully for comfort.

When the office had been reached he shut and locked the door, a fact of which Trixie took note and her heart beat harder than ever. She settled uneasily into a chair and watched Tarlton as he threw off his hat and then considered her, hands deep in his trouser pockets.

'How much did you tell Smoke Cavendish?' he asked briefly, and Trixie's grey eyes looked at him in sudden fear.

'Tell him? When?'

'Tonight when you left. You should never have come back, Trix . . . I'm not a fool,' Tarlton went on, his eyes pitiless. 'You found out this evening that the story of a marshal was a fake, didn't you? — and the first thing you did when you found that out was to go

165

running to your erstwhile boyfriend, Smoke Cavendish!'

'No!' Trixie retorted flatly, choosing a lie as the only means of escape. 'I — I didn't do anything like that — '

'You've overlooked something, Trix,' Tarlton continued. 'Seated at that saddle-tramp's table there was a cattle dealer. I had a talk with him afterwards, when I was trying to find out things about the fire and your attacker. He told me what the saddle-tramp had been saying — So it all adds up. You went running, then like the damned little fool you are you came back. Why? To try and run with both sides, or what?'

Trixie was breathing heavily, trying not to show fear, and doing it very badly. Tarlton took his hands out of his pockets and unbuckled the heavy gun belt from about his waist. With a deliberate action he tipped out the cartridges on to the table and then put the gun away in his desk drawer. This done he twined the belt partly up his arm and left one end of it swinging in his hand.

'I'll stand anything from a woman except a rebound,' he said slowly. 'To come back here and pretend to be with me, part of me, sharing my secrets and everything, when you're selling everything back to Smoke Cavendish, is more than I mean to take. I'm hounding you out of town, Trixie — if there's enough of you left to ever get out. I'm settling the issue straight and clear. You've finished with me — but good, and here's your receipt for the double-cross!'

The tail end of his belt whipped out and slashed with brutal force across Trixie's face as she jumped to her feet. She screamed with the pain of it and twisted round, her hands to her eyes. Instantly the belt came again, blasting through her thin, expensive dress and cutting it to shreds. Blood began to streak in the torn fabric.

'I reckon you'd tell him everything you ever learned,' Tarlton continued, his voice steel-hard. 'Probably about my planning to wipe him out, probably about my ditching his timber — Been a nice little go-between, haven't you? After this you can crawl where you like as long as it ain't here!'

Trixie turned, quivering, pain eating into her flayed back. Her face was livid red from ear to chin where the belt had struck her. Suddenly she made a dive for the desk where she remembered Tarlton had put his gun, then she gasped in anguish as the belt caught up with her.

Back and forth it slashed across her back — four times, five, six, seven, and with each murderous blow she could feel the life dying inside her. She turned dizzily, and the belt hit her across the throat. It seemed to her that fire drowned her breathing. She sank helplessly and thudded to the floor, arms sprawling, blonde hair tangled.

Tarlton breathed hard, perspiration rolling down his face. He stared at the savage cuts on the girl's now bare back, then hc put his belt back on again slowly, returned the cartridges and gun to their rightful places.

'Reckon there's something gets me sometimes,' he muttered, hand to his forehead. 'Just plain murder when I'm crossed. Can't seem to figger it . . . ' He got a grip on himself and staggered over to the rolltop. From inside it he took a brandy bottle and poured out a stiff drink. Having tossed it back he stood breathing hard and recovering. He had not had such a fit of temper as this since . . . When? Yes, it had been in Denver. Been uncontrollable, building up, until he'd had to kill to ease the pressure.

At length he returned to the girl and hauled up her limp form to a standing position, her head lolling against his shoulder. Holding her to him he dragged out one of her own overcoats from the nearby cupboard and drew it over her shoulders, buttoning it in front. Then he heaved her over his broad shoulder and opened the window.

In a moment or two he had slid down the veranda roof and dragged the girl after him. He had only one thing in his mind now — to be rid of her, to silence her so she could not recover and speak of what had happened to her this night. The coat would keep bloodstains from his hands, and she could just disappear . . . only it was not that easy. As he laid her unconscious body by the side of the boardwalk, preparatory to getting his horse from the back of the saloon, four men came out of the front door of the Hell's Acres.

Tarlton glanced about him desperately, but the time was too short for him to move the girl and himself — so he ran for it into the shadows at the side of the building and crouched there, waiting to see what happened next.

The men, none of them under the weather, couldn't possibly miss the girl's silent figure. They looked at each other in amazement, then bent down and examined her. It was only the work of a moment or two to unfasten her coat and discover the brutal savagery with which she had been attacked.

'Looks like a job fur the sheriff,' one of the men said, his face grim. 'I don't reckon t'know who did this but I'd sure like to tear out his liver.'

Another of the men glanced about him. 'I guess she only lives across the street there, at Ma Bradshaw's. Better take her in there. Sheriff lives there, too. One of yuh had better nip back into the Hell's Acres here and tell the boss. He'll be mighty burned up to know what's happened to his girl-friend.'

Tarlton swore to himself and immediately began a hasty shinning up one of the supporting pillars at the back of the saloon, the only possible way by which he could return to his office. Meantime the unconscious Trixie was carried reverently by the remaining three cow-punchers into Ma Bradshaw's rooming-house, and she gave a gasp of horror as the limp form was laid down on the sofa in the main living-room and the lacerated back was exposed to view.

'Git Smoke!' she ordered, her voice venomous. 'An' tell Flossie t'git in here pronto with a bowl of warm water, bandages, and a sponge. Hurry up, you lugs!' she yelled, as the men stood staring, and that jumped them into activity.

Flossie — Ma Bradshaw's only daughter — arrived promptly enough. Between them, she and her mother set to work to remove the blood and apply the bandages. They were half-way through it, Trixie sprawled face down and still senseless on the couch when Smoke came into the room. He took one look at the girl, naked to the waist, her half-bandaged back exposed, then his jaws tightened.

'Any idea who did this?' he demanded of the men, but they shook their heads.

'Just found her lying outside the Hell's Acres, sheriff, just like she'd been dumped. Her face is pretty well knocked about too — '

Smoke reached out his hand to take a look at the girl's features, but Ma

Bradshaw stopped him.

'No yuh don't, Smoke. She ain't decent in front. Take my word fur it — her face is badly cut about.'

Smoke nodded then took out his gun and snapped it open. With a decisive click he reclosed it and returned it to its holster.

'I'll be back,' he said tautly, and strode into the hall.

'Hey — wait a minnit!' Ma sprang to her feet. 'Come back here, Smoke — Flossie, git on with that bandaging. You fellas can scram: this is a job fur women. And you come inter the kitchen, Smoke.'

'Not me, Ma, I've an appointment — '

'Come here!' Ma roared. 'Yuh may be a sheriff but I'm old enough t'be yuh mother — Git inter that kitchen!'

Smoke hesitated, then with an irritated movement obeyed the order. Ma came waddling in after him and closed the door.

'Where did yuh figger on goin', son?' she demanded.

'To put six bullets straight through Mark Tarlton's heart!' Smoke retorted. 'And the sooner I go, the better!'

'I thought that wus your intention, Smoke — but what good is it goin' t'do yuh?'

'Oh, quit stalling, Ma!' Smoke got to his feet impatiently. 'I've got a job to do — '

'Mebbe, but do you *know* Mark Tarlton's back of this business with Trixie?'

'Not to swear on it, but I reckon nothing's more sure. Trixie went back to him tonight to spy for me. If he'd found that out it would account for him beatin' her up as he has — and I'm going to pay him out for it. Kill him, if I can.'

'Yuh actin' more like a tarnation fool than a sheriff,' Ma said frankly. 'If Tarlton did beat Trixie up he'll know yuh'll come gunnin' fur him and he'll be ready. He'll blast yuh before you can get near him. If he didn't do it, and you shoot him dead — what does that make you? A killer, son, no matter how yuh look at it.'

Smoke tightened his lips for a moment. 'None of which alters the fact that I've got to avenge Trixie!'

'The thing's simple enough, Smoke, if yuh'd stop bein' so hot-headed. Wait till she gets her wits back and can tell yuh what happened. It ain't as if she's dead. She'll be okay in time. When yuh know the facts yuh can act. No more'n a matter of hours. Worth it to be sure. Then yuh can think coolly.'

Smoke's blazing fury began to subside a little. He gave a grim smile and patted Ma's fat shoulder.

'OK, Ma, you're right. Let's get back and see how she's going on.'

They turned into the living-room to find that Flossie had completed all of the bandaging and wrapped Trixie up in a heavy gown. She lay on her back now, breathing shallowly, the weals across her face hidden by carefully taped bandages and wadding.

'Suppose we ought to get Doc Jones?'

Smoke asked. 'He once fixed me up good.'

Ma shook her head. 'Nothin' he can do that we can't. I reckon the only thing now is fur Trixie to lie abed until she gets her wits back. Looks like the shock of the attack has knocked her out cold. Better get her up to her room.'

Smoke nodded. The cowpunchers who had brought the girl in from the street had gone now, so it was left to Smoke to carry the girl upstairs. He did it — reverently — laid her on the bed, and left the rest to Ma and Flossie. There was nothing more he could do now but wait for Trixie to return to consciousness and explain who had attacked her.

Altogether, Smoke passed a restless night — bobbing into the girl's room at intervals to learn that she had not yet recovered. When morning came she was still dead out so Smoke made it his business to fetch Dr. Jones.

'Shock,' he said, after he had made an examination. 'And it acts in different ways with different people. She may recover any minute, or it may take a long time: no way of telling.'

'Any danger?' Smoke asked anxiously.

'I guess not. Flossie here's done a good job of bandaging and Trixie's healthy enough to recover rapidly once she gets her senses back . . . Just let Nature take its course, I guess.'

So there was nothing for Smoke to do but control his impatience until Trixie became conscious again . . . but he had other matters to attend to. Urgent ones. And immediately after breakfast he went about the town summoning those men who were on his side and gathering them in the empty building.

'Boys, we're fighting Tarlton from here on with all we've got,' he announced. 'He's on to our plans, and he had poor Clayburn killed in order to get the information — but we can't do anything to him without proof.'

'I don't see that, sheriff,' one of the men snapped, his hand on his gun. 'Let's go get that critter an' never mind th' reg'lashuns.'

Smoke shook his head. 'No. I realize how you feel, but as sheriff I'm compelled to uphold the law. Give Tarlton enough time and he'll hang himself. I also think he's responsible for having Trixie Lee beaten up last night, but I can't prove that either until she recovers consciousness and talks . . . Anyways, I got you here for another reason. We're riding out to Jetmore Pass to put a stop to Tarlton's boys trying to ditch our timber. Trixie warned me about that, so we've got to act. Get your horses and we'll be on our way.'

The men did not hesitate. The call to action was just what they wanted and within ten minutes the round dozen of them were mounted and heading out of town with Smoke at their head. He had taken care to leave by the back route so that Tarlton, if on the watch — a more than likely possibility — would not be able to suspect things.

The journey to Jetmore was a good seventy-five miles, but since the hour was still early and the train from Dodge

City was not expected to pass Jetmore until around three o'clock, there was time to make the trip, with halts.

The character of the country changed as the men rode onwards. The sandy trail gave place to more rocky regions as they came within sight of a line of hills. They stopped for a meal on the outskirts of the hills, and then pushed on steadily until they had gained a point where they could see the solitary railroad track leading through a natural cutting.

'Reckon we're around a mile from Jetmore itself, sheriff, and the pass,' one of the men said. 'Since we haven't seen any of Tarlton's boys I guess they must have started before us. I guess they wouldn't leave it this late to get themselves in position. Train's due in thirty minutes.'

'Unless I miss my guess Tarlton's boys will be a good way from here,' Smoke said. 'The only way they can ditch our timber at the pass there' — and he indicated a narrow spot where a bridge crossed a ravine — 'is to board the train some time ahead. Best thing we can do is to get to the other side of that pass and then open up if we see them at work. No punches pulled, remember. If those men are aboard that train they're trespassers, and the law says we can shoot 'em down. And we will! Now come on . . . '

He swung round his horse's head and darted the animal down the long, rocky slope which led to flatter ground. After that he kept on going steadily until — by a circuitous route — he had gained the end of the ravine bridge with his men behind him. They crossed it, using the railroad itself as a track, then at a point a mile beyond it they turned off the railroad and into the surrounding cliffs. Ultimately they had reached a spot where they could see the railroad clearly, and where they also had a clear stretch down which to drive the horses into action.

'Right,' Smoke said, relaxing on the saddle horn. 'I guess this is it. Nothing to do now but wait . . . '

There was silence for a moment. Only the glaring sun, the blaze of the grey rocks, the hot wind. Then a thought seemed to strike one of the men.

'Isn't it possible, sheriff, that Tarlton may suspect you know what he aims to do, and will have called off his stunt?'

'More than possible,' Smoke answered him. 'But it means a lot to Tarlton to stop our timber reaching Hell's Acres so I think he'll go ahead and risk attack. It's the only move he can make right now — '

'Here she comes!' another of the men interrupted, pointing into the distance.

Smoke narrowed his eyes towards a white plume curling far away in the sunlight. Faintly, on the still air, came the mournful clanging of the locomotive's bell. Then as the train began to come nearer it was revealed as a long freight caterpillar, twining in and out of the rocks.

'Okay,' Smoke said presently. 'Let's get down to ground level . . . '

His men immediately followed after him, sweeping down the slope and drawing to a halt within the shadow of a rock spur. From here they could see the oncoming train, but could not be seen themselves. Out of sight, a considerable distance away to their left, was the ravine. According to Smoke's calculations there was time to stop any dirty work before the ravine could be reached, assuming that the timber would be on an open freight wagon.

Its bell still clanging vigorously, steam belching into the hot air, the locomotive came past, followed by its long string of wagons. Intently, Smoke and his men watched — then as the seventh wagon came rumbling past they beheld three men crouched upon it, busily at work on the chains which were holding not only planed timber direct from a sawmill, but also immense logs. From the look of things the plan was to empty the entire wagon by letting the chain loose.

'After 'em!' Smoke ordered, and

spurred his horse forward.

He did not attempt to catch the timber wagon itself. He rode alongside the wagon which happened to be nearest and then vaulted to it from his saddle. Gun in his right hand, using his left to steady himself, he leapt quickly from truck to truck, finishing the rocky journey on the roof of a cattle truck. He yanked out his second gun and aimed both of them at the men on the timber wagon.

'Hold it!' he ordered. 'Any more monkey business with those chains and you get both barrels!'

The men directly below stopped their activities. Apparently there were about six of them all told, three on one side and three on the other — but though they stopped working on the chains they snatched at their guns. Smoke fired instantly and then flung himself down. His bullet sent one man reeling from the wagon to the rock at the side of the trail. At the same instant a return slug split the woodwork of the truck close by Smoke's head.

Then his own men had wormed along to join him and shots exploded back and forth.

'Keep 'em occupied,' Smoke ordered, dodging up and firing, then ducking down again. 'Once we've gotten past that ravine there won't be any point in 'em ditching that timber. It'll only fall at the wayside and we can figger out means of getting it later. We'd never get it out of the ravine, though — '

More woodwork splintered. A man close to Smoke gave a howl of pain, dropped his gun, then rolled from the truck roof and vanished. Smoke's eyes glinted. He peeped up, took aim, and fired. He got his mark as one of the men below twisted round, clutching at his middle. He made a frantic effort to save himself, missed, and fell over the edge of the wagon just as it came to the ravine. There was a vision of his body hurtling down into the narrow depths.

Evidently realizing that the shooting match could go on indefinitely, and that it was no longer any use trying to ditch the timber, the men below made frantic leaps outward the moment the ravine had been crossed. Smoke motioned those beside him to hold their fire.

'Waste of bullets,' he said. 'We've stopped them doing anything, and that's all that counts. We may as well go with the train into Hell's Acres itself. Jerry will bring in the horses.'

'Unless those gun-hawks find him,' one of the men said. 'If that happens we'll lose the horses, and Jerry.'

'He can look after himself,' Smoke said, quite confident. 'It certainly isn't worth our while to skip this loco and then walk all the way back — as those mugs will have to do to their own horses. They might even get on the train again at the end,' he added. 'Better be on the watch for them . . .'

But the gunmen did not reappear. Evidently they had had enough.

7

By the afternoon the freight train had arrived at Hell's Acres. Smoke promptly commandeered what buckboards he could find and the timber was transported to the interior of his potential saloon. This done he called for, and got, volunteers to guard the place; then he hurried to Ma Bradshaw's to satisfy himself on the one subject constantly worrying him . . . Trixie.

'Yeah, she's recovered,' Ma Bradshaw told him, the moment he questioned her. 'She got her senses back not half an hour after yuh'd gone this morning. Won't be long before she's around again. I've fixed her up with good soup and she's bin asleep most uv the day.'

'Okay if I go up and see her?' Smoke questioned.

Ma nodded, so he sped quickly up the stairs to Trixie's room. He found her awake, propped up in pillows, looking through the half opened window on to the dusty main street.

'Trix . . . ' Smoke hurried forward and sat on the edge of the bed, grasping her hand. 'Ma's been telling me; you're getting better.'

Trixie nodded slowly. The bandage which had been across her face had been removed now, but the ugly red sears which the belt had inflicted were still there, inflamed but slowly healing.

'Feeling more — okay?' Smoke prompted, anxiously.

'I'll be all right, Smoke.' Her grey eyes studied him. 'I guess I owe the fact that I'm in a good bed in a safe house entirely to you — and those men who carried me in. I don't think Mark ever intended it to work out like that.'

'Then it was him! I guessed as much. I was all set for beating the daylights out of him, only Ma stopped me until I had exact proof. Now I've got it . . . ' Smoke clenched his fists and for a moment sat looking across the street at the closed saloon.

'I think he meant to kill me,' Trixie added, shuddering. 'I couldn't stand him thrashing me any longer, so I collapsed. I don't remember any more. I can't think why he ditched me where I could be found — unless he got scared.'

'Not half so scared as he's going to be,' Smoke said, brooding.

'He guessed everything,' Trixie muttered. 'Naturally, that's the end of my trying to learn anything for you — What about the timber? Did you save it?'

'I sure did, thanks to you. Tarlton's boys were crawling over it like flies but we stopped 'em. Right now the stuff's in my building and we go to work getting it ready at the earliest moment. I'll sure give Tarlton a run for his money before he's finished — if he's still alive then.' Smoke got to his feet. 'I'm going to have a clean up, a meal, and then attend to some business,' he added.

'Mark will be expecting you, Smoke!' The girl's grey eyes were anxious. 'And he'll be doubly furious when he hears that he hasn't ditched your timber. Wouldn't it be safer to leave him alone?'

'And excuse the hell he gave you? Sorry, Trix, I'm not made that way.'

She protested again, but Smoke would not listen. He stooped and kissed her and then left the room — and across the street Tarlton had just arrived for the night's business. He took good care, however, to drive his buckboard round to the back of the saloon. Knowing his own tactics he had the fear that somebody might snipe at him from Ma Bradshaw's and he wasn't taking that chance. In fact he was deeply puzzled. He had expected trouble from Smoke long before this. The thought of Trixie unconscious for so long a time had never occurred to him.

His complacency was shaken somewhat when, an hour later, one of his gunhawks came into his office. Tarlton eyed him, turning from the mirror where he had been adjusting his shoestring tie.

'Well, get rid of that timber?' he asked briefly.

'No.' The puncher gave a look under his eyes. 'I guess your hunch was right, boss. Trixie Lee musta tipped off the sheriff: he wus waitin' for us. We had to get off the train.'

'I figgered that might happen . . . ' Tarlton rubbed his chin for a moment and then shrugged. 'Okay, since that's what happened, I can deal with the sheriff in other ways. He'll sure not build that saloon he's aiming at. I s'pose he's back in town now?'

'Sure. Got all his timber in the building — so Jeff says. He's bin on watch.'

'Which means he may be coming here next. Once Trixie talks I'm expecting trouble. Let me know the moment he shows up. I'm not going into the saloon tonight; I want a chance to protect myself and here's the best place. If he does come it'll be a good chance for you and the boys to get busy.'

'Doin' what?' the gunhawk questioned.

'I want that building of his burned to the ground,' Tarlton snapped. 'Since he's out, with his timber in there, it's a good chance to get rid of the lot at one go. We can't attempt it unless we know exactly where he is, otherwise we might be caught out. But if he comes to see me we'll know where he is — then you and the boys can get busy. Got that?'

'Okay,' the gunhawk assented. 'I'll see it's done.'

He left the office and Tarlton took up a position behind his desk. Instead of leaving his gun in its holster he took it into his hand in readiness. He did not feel safe. He knew that Smoke might come at any moment, but it could hardly be by any other means than the door or window.

Smoke, however, had a pretty good idea of Tarlton's state of mind and was prepared for difficulties in dealing with him. Before he left Ma Bradshaw's after his bath and meal he spent half an hour removing one of the long wires from his bed mattress and carefully unplaiting it until he had five thin flexible steel wires. These he bound tightly with twine to the top of an old shaving brush handle. The whole villainous thing fitted comfortably in his trouser pocket and gave no hint of his intentions when he eventually walked into the Hell's Acres in mid-evening.

The eyes of Tarlton's boys, lounging in various parts of the big room, followed his progress to the bar. He ordered whiskey and then glanced about him.

'Where's Tarlton?' he asked the barkeep.

'Dunno, sheriff. Ain't seen him since he arrived. Must be busy in his office, I guess.'

'Tell him I want a word with him. It's important.'

The barkeep hesitated, then seeing Smoke's determined face he left his duties to the other barmen and ducked under the counter's far end. Smoke, instead of bothering with his whiskey, began to follow him. Puzzled, the 'boys' in the pool room looked at one another, undecided what to do.

Unaware he was being dogged so closely the barman went to the office door and knocked.

'You there, Mr Tarlton?' he asked.

'Yeah,' came faintly to Smoke's ears. 'What is it?'

'I guess — ' The barman stopped, a gun in his back.

'Tell him to open the door. You've private information.' Smoke's voice was only a whisper, but it had infinite meaning.

'Well, what is it?' Tarlton barked from beyond the door.

'I'm — I'm not rightly in a position t'shout this through a door, boss. It's private.'

Tarlton muttered something impatiently, then the door bolt snapped back. He began to open the door and the next second a sledgehammer fist struck him in the face. With a howl of pain he hurtled backwards, collided with the desk, then fell to the floor. For a second or two he was too dazed to realize what had happened. He breathed hard, wiped blood from his cut lip with the back of his hand, and then looked up. He found Smoke with his back to the door, his arms folded.

'Get up,' he ordered, his voice intensely quiet.

Slowly Tarlton did so, his eyes travelling to the gun which had been knocked out of his hand when he'd keeled over. Smoke eyed him with an unblinking stare.

'Locked yourself in, huh?' he asked. 'I guessed you would. Simple enough to get the barman to make you open up.'

Tarlton waited, his fists clenched. Smoke still did not move.

'I'm a sheriff,' he said, 'and as such I could jail you for what you did to Trixie Lee — but I'm 'not interested in locking you up. That's no punishment for a rat like you. So right now I'm not a sheriff but just an ordinary guy who doesn't like the way you treat a woman.' Smoke tugged off his sheriff's badge and tossed it on the nearby desk. 'This is unofficial,' he explained. 'If I kill you it's up to the populace to say what shall be done with me when they've heard the full facts.'

Tarlton frowned a little, wondering what was coming.

'I've also a bit of added repayment to make for your trying to ditch my timber, though having got it through safely I'm not much bothered. It's Trixie I'm thinking of — the hell you gave her. You figgered on killing her, I guess, only something stopped you.'

'So what?' Mark Tarlton demanded. 'Wouldn't you do the same to a dame if she ratted on you? You can't — '

Tarlton broke off and dived for his gun, and it was then that Smoke's right hand flashed out of his pocket and brought the five steel lashes down across Tarlton's back. He gasped and turned, not particularly hurt because of the thickness of his jacket. He clenched his fist to aim a savage blow, and that was when the lashes really got him. They wrapped round his wrist and knuckles and bit deep, bringing blood quickly.

'Why, you dirty — ' Tarlton lunged with all his strength, jerking his head back with a cry of anguish as the tails bit across his face, adding a further cut to his already damaged lip.

'That's for the one in the face you gave Trixie,' Smoke explained, as the agonized Tarlton lurched back and forth, clutching at his cheeks. 'I'll leave your face out of it from here on and make up for the rest.'

From his belt Smoke whipped out his knife and slashed it quickly up the back of Tarlton's coat. It fell apart and left him with only the satin back of his fancy waistcoat, and shirt, for protection.

Smoke did not wield his whip with blind passion. He swung it with deliberate strokes, and each lash sent the pain-racked Tarlton staggering dizzily. Finally he collapsed half sobbing in a corner and made no attempt to rise.

'That's all,' Smoke said, his voice at the same level. 'I guess you'll recover more quickly than Trixie did because you've a tougher constitution. That's something I can't help. If you try anything else you'll get it repaid.'

Smoke picked up his badge and put it in his pocket, then he left the office and slammed the door. He felt a good deal better with Trixie avenged. Without looking to right or left he made his way through the saloon and then paused for a moment at the sight of the unusual crowd round the gaming table. He began to drift that way.

His guess that maybe Carmichael was at it again was correct. The fat gambler was sitting back in his chair, cheroot smouldering, watching the spinning wheel. In front of him was a stack of chips and wads of notes. He glanced up once as he saw Smoke, grinned significantly, and then returned his attention to his play.

'Guess this must be Tarlton's unlucky night,' Smoke murmured to himself, then he went on his way again.

The moment he reached the board-walk he came to an abrupt halt, staring fixedly across the street. Flames were soaring from the dark bulk of the building he had bought and smoke was surging across the main street in billowing clouds. Around the building a gathering of men and women was doing its utmost with an endless chain to get the fire under control.

Smoke swung back into the saloon quickly.

'Hey everybody!' he shouted. 'Fire! Quickly, all of you! We've got to get it down before the whole town catches alight.'

It was not so much Smoke's authority as sheriff which brought a response as the fear of the people for their own homes . . . Those who were not too absorbed in the game being played by Carmichael hurtled towards the batwings, and in a moment or two a surging crowd of men and women augmented the few who were fighting the flames.

As sheriff, Smoke took over. Since it was quite obvious that his own building had no chance he concentrated on the buildings surrounding it, having them saturated with water and cutting away all possible timber connections by which the fire might spread. At the end of an hour the conflagration was under control, but all that remained of Smoke's building, and the assayer's office which had been next to it, was a black smouldering pile of ash.

Exhausted, sweat streaked, the men and women began to drift away, satisfied that the battle was won. For a long time Smoke stood studying the utter ruin of his hopes, then he wandered into Ma Bradshaw's and went upstairs wearily. Knocking on Trixie's door he received an answer from Ma Bradshaw herself.

She was standing at the window of the bedroom looking out on the kerosene-lighted street. Trixie was propped up in the bed, the bed drawn round so that she too could see outside. She turned her head sharply as Smoke entered.

'Smoke, what's been happening?' Trixie asked quickly. 'We saw the fire — as well as we could from this sharp angle. Is it under control?'

'Yeah.' Smoke pulled up a chair and sat down heavily. He tossed his hat down on the nearby table. 'No more danger — and no more building for me either!'

'Y'mean that hall you'd figgered on havin' has been burned down?' Ma asked blankly.

'Every bit of it, and the timber inside it. I've lost the lot — and naturally Tarlton's back of it. I had a man watching the building but I don't suppose Tarlton's boys would find it very difficult to deal with him. Must have happened whilst I was dealing with Tarlton.'

'What — did you do to him?' Trixie asked quietly.

'I flayed him wide open, Trix — gave him back everything he gave you — hundred per cent.' Smoke looked before him moodily. 'Not that I get much satisfaction out of it now. He pulled another fast one even whilst I was doing it.'

'This means yuh'll have ter rebuild,' Ma said.

'With what? I used up nearly all the money on buying the building and getting the new timber. Carmichael wouldn't be such an idiot as to finance me again. I've some money left and I still own the land on which that building stood — but that's precious little consolation . . . Yeah, who is it?' Smoke broke off, as there was a knock on the door.

It was one of his puncher friends who entered. He pulled off his hat awkwardly.

'I guess Flossie told me yuh wus up here, sheriff. I thought I'd better let yuh know what happened at the building.'

'It burned down. I know that much.'

'I was guarding it,' the puncher said. 'I didn't stand a chance. Six men rushed on me and flattened me out. When I came to I was lying in the grass some way from the building and it was in flames. I helped with the other folks ter try and stop the fire, but I'd no chance to talk to yuh then. So — I'm here. Just tellin' yuh.'

Smoke gave a shrug. 'Okay, Bill — thanks. Nothing you could do against that, I reckon. This is one round to Tarlton.'

'Yeah — looks that way. I guess there's a round he ain't winning, though, an' that's over at the Hell's Acres. The fat man's takin' him for a ride.'

'I noticed that as I left.'

'Yuh should see it now,' the puncher grinned. 'The fat man's cleaned out Tarlton's bank and now he's gambling with Tarlton's property. If this goes on Tarlton'll be cleaned out of everything he's got! I only just came frum the saloon. Went in to cool off after the fire.'

'This sounds as though it might be interesting,' Smoke said, after reflection. 'Guess I might go over and see if Carmichael gets in the mood to help me again, though I think he'd be crazy if he did. I'll be back,' he added, with a glance at Ma and Trixie. 'With some good news, mebbe.'

The puncher beside him he went across the main street and re-entered the Hell's Acres. He had never seen the tables so empty. All the men and women, and for that matter the barmen too, were gathered in a circle round the main gambling table. The proceedings there were hidden, but there was the sound of the ball clicking and then a gasp from the spectators.

Smoke eased his way through the crowd until he had gained a front position. He saw Carmichael at the table, his winnings piled around him. A harassed looking banker was standing by, his resources exhausted. Only the croupier remained dead-pan, ready for action. Carmichael was greasy and smoking steadily, his sleeves rolled up past his plump elbows. Nearby stood Tarlton himself, dressed again, moving with obvious pain, a plaster disfiguring his face where the whip had caught him. Round one wrist was a bandage. It said much for his immense stamina that he tolerated clothes over his raw back.

'Twenty seven,' the croupier said, as the wheel ceased spinning. 'You win again, Mr Carmichael.'

Carmichael grinned and looked around him, then up towards Smoke.

'Hello there, sheriff. Glad yuh lookin' on. I'm sure givin' Tarlton plenty to worry over. I've won six main street buildings frum him and all his bank.'

Tarlton glanced up and met Smoke's bleak stare. For a second the two men measured each other, then Carmichael spoke again.

'I'm feelin' lucky and I ain't finished,' he said deliberately. 'What else are you gamblin', Tarlton? I figger you're not the kind of guy to let all this go without a fight to get it back?'

Tarlton looked about him. If he refused to gamble any further with a customer it would not do his business any good. If on the other hand he did gamble and lost matters might become desperate. He was thinking it out when Carmichael spoke again.

'Tell you what I'll do, Tarlton. This lucky streak of mine can't last much longer. I'll stake all this pile, and the properties I've won from you, and this saloon of yours. If I win on the next round I keep the lot, including the saloon. If I lose you get everything and keep your saloon. How's that?'

There was silence. Tarlton moved uneasily and winced. He saw the faces turned towards him. Was he gambler enough to risk everything or too yellow to take the final chance? If he lost it meant the end of his rulership of Hell's Acres. If he won he'd be more powerful than ever —

'OK,' he said briefly. 'It's a deal.'

Carmichael rubbed his hands and pushed everything he had got on the number 15. Nobody knew why, since he had been playing on 27 most of the evening, with occasional variations — but evidently he had his own mathematical system. The wheel began spinning and the ball clicked. The wheel seemed to spin for an interminable time, then at last began to slow down.

Slower — slower — it halted.

'Fifteen,' announced the croupier phlegmatically, and raised his eyes to Tarlton.

The spectators sighed. Tarlton looked about him, trying not to show how shaken he was. He had no chance of escaping his obligations, either, with so many people around him.

'OK, you win,' he said. 'I'll get you the deeds for this place and make them over to you — Luke Bairstow here?' he asked, looking into the crowd.

The lawyer came forward, something approaching dismay on his lean face.

The disappearance of his boss as a power in the district would have nasty repercussions on him, too.

'You've got the deeds, Bairstow,' Tarlton told him. 'Get them, and make out a transfer. Hurry it up.'

The lawyer departed into the crowd again, presumably on his way to his office. Carmichael sat breathing hard and considering.

'I guess you'll need a manager for this place,' Tarlton said, after a while. 'Nobody better than me. I know all the ropes.'

'I've already gotten myself a manager,' Carmichael replied, glancing up. 'I'm putting the sheriff there in charge of this saloon place, as some kind of recompense for losing his own saloon. He had a good idea there, and you smashed it up, Tarlton.'

'You're a dirty liar!' Tarlton flared.

'No I'm not. I heard the people around me even if I was playin'. I gathered enough to know Smoke Cavendish's place had been burned out, and no critter would do that 'cept you. That's why I took you up for all you've got, an' also because my money was tied up in that building you destroyed. I reckon it's better to have a ready made place like this than have to build one. And a sheriff as manager will keep order — and prevent any crooked wheels.'

Tarlton scowled, but this time he did not say anything.

'And Trixie Lee will come back here, too,' Carmichael continued. 'She'll be in good hands with Smoke behind her. You can get out, Tarlton, when you've handed over those deeds. You're finished. From here on I'm boss of Hell's Acres. I've got the saloon and all bar two of your properties an' most of your money. You can get out — and good riddance.'

Smoke gave Carmichael a look of gratitude and the fat man smiled; then he sat waiting and smoking steadily until Bairstow came back with the deeds and transfer. Tarlton signed, and the croupier witnessed; then Tarlton threw down the pen savagely and turned away. He would probably have moved with angry strides only his flayed back would not let him. Instead he crept, heading for his office.

'You serious about this?' Smoke asked quietly, and the fat man grinned widely.

'Never more serous in my life. Y'know, I've taken quite a fancy to Hell's Acres. Turned out t'be one of the luckiest places I was ever in. I guess we can have a new deal all round with Tarlton outa the way.'

Most of the men and women present nodded promptly enough, but others — particularly those who had stood to gain a good deal by Tarlton's dictatorship of the district — began to sidle out of the pool room and vanished beyond the batwings.

'Tomorrow we'll talk business,' Smoke said, turning away. 'Right now I'm heading back to tell Trixie the news, and also to keep an eye on her in case

Tarlton tries anything. I can't see him taking a beating like this lying down, and he might vent his spleen on Trixie . . . Be seeing you.'

'You sure will, son. And tell Trixie to hurry up and get well. This place needs her to cheer it up.'

8

The following day Tarlton had departed from the district — or at least from Hell's Acres itself. There were reports from those who had watched his movements that he had retired to his ranch, taking with him those few men who still believed they had something to gain by being loyal to him.

To Smoke, the whole thing was a puzzle. He had expected a violent reaction — yet there didn't seem to be one. For a week he and his boys were on the alert, but nothing happened, so it began to look as though Tarlton knew when he was beaten and wasn't intending to stick his chin out.

At the end of the week Trixie returned to the Hell's Acres in her former capacity, but with a lighter heart. Though her back was still not healed enough to permit the wearing of low cut gowns she was present amongst the customers, and that seemed to be all they wanted. She felt perfectly safe with Smoke always at hand, ready to deal with any man who got out of line.

On the whole, Smoke had nothing to grumble about. Carmichael was paying him well to run the place and he also had his official money as sheriff. In a town so small as Hell's Acres, however, and with a troublemaker like Tarlton removed, there was little demand for his services as sheriff. It was at best a part-time job. So when he was not in the saloon or attending to his few duties as sheriff he was helping Carmichael in property deals by which the fat gambler could acquire, by degrees, a complete hold of the town. Such was his nature, he would probably gamble the lot one night and lose it.

It was about a month after Smoke had taken over the management of the Hell's Acres when something happened to disturb the uneasy peace which had descended on the area. Towards mid-evening, when the saloon was well settled down to its business, a saddle-tramp came in — or rather staggered in. He was smothered in trail dust, his clothes torn, two days' stubble on his leathery face. Certainly he was not a man anybody present recognized. He was watched as he half tottered to the bar, then he looked up as Smoke gave him a helpful hand.

'What's the matter, fella?' he asked, surprised. 'Been havin' a brush with outlaws or something?'

'Nope, I reckon not, sheriff. I jus' happened on somethin' I can't rightly believe — Give me brandy quick, then I'll tell you.'

The barkeep handed it over and the saddle tramp downed it quickly. The men and women continued to look at him. Trixie drifted over interestedly.

'I found a — a bonanza,' the tramp said, and then he gave a start as he realized he had perhaps spoken too loudly. The stares of the men and women had become intense.

'Congratulations,' Smoke said. 'You're a prospector then?'

'Yeah, sure, 'Scratch' Maloney they call me. I'm from Arizony. Biggest bonanza yuh ever saw, sheriff an' no more'n ten miles north uv here — '

'Take it easy, Scratch,' Smoke interrupted, glancing about him. 'Any more talk that loud and you'll have a bonanza no longer. Don't you know better than to talk about gold in that give-away fashion?'

'Where is it, fella?' a puncher shouted, leaping up. 'Yuh can't keep a whole bonanza to yourself!'

'Nope, that ain't right.' Another man jumped up. 'Where is it?'

'Don't say a word,' Smoke cautioned, as the prospector looked about him worriedly.

'Why not? I reckon there's enough gold an' t'spare fur everybody. Fact I'll show yuh!' Scratch Maloney began to wave his arms violently. 'Durned if I want all that yeller metal fur myself

. . . It's ten miles out, along rough country. That's how I got inter this mess. Come with me an' I'll show yuh.'

Such an offer had probably never been made in the history of Hell's Acres — or even in the whole history of the West. For a prospector to be willing to share his bonanza with a horde of get-rich-quicks was unheard of. It certainly started pandemonium in the saloon. The men and women went bundling over each other to reach the batwings, carrying Scratch Maloney along in their midst. At magical speed the place emptied, even to the barmen. At last only Smoke and Trixie were left behind — then they saw that Carmichel was present too at a distant table, finishing off his drink.

'Bum steer,' he said, glancing across.

'You're right,' Smoke agreed grimly. 'About one of the neatest gags I've struck in some time. No prospector who isn't loco would tell far and wide about a strike: it's a draw off, to take every man and woman out of town.

They'll be away for some time, probably, looking for that imaginary gold mine — '

'Imaginary?' Trixie repeated in surprise. 'You mean it ain't genuine?'

'Not a word of it, Trix.'

'Then where's the sense of it?'

'Tarlton,' Smoke said, his lips tight. 'That add up? How to get hold of this saloon and clear everybody out — Why, just mention the word gold and you can empty the place quicker than with a plague . . . Only I'm not falling for it. And neither have you, Carmichael.'

'I figger it like you,' Carmichael responded. 'And anyways I don't need gold. I've an easier way of making money.'

Smoke took out his guns and examined them, then he hurried over to the batwings and looked outside. The main street was as empty as though Hell's Acres were a ghost town. He stepped back into the saloon and closed the main doors behind the batwings, then he crossed over to the hanging lamps and quickly extinguished them. At length the place was in darkness.

'Now what?' Trixie asked uneasily from the blackness.

'If it is Tarlton back of this he'll pull something very soon,' Smoke told her, his hand taking her arm. He'll probably know that I won't fall for a gag like a gold strike: his one object is to take away all the support I could have got from the townspeople, so we — '

He broke off. Suddenly one of the windows had splintered under the impact of a bullet from outside. When the tinkle of the glass had died away a voice became audible — unmistakably Tarlton's.

'If anybody's in that saloon, they'd better come out with their hands up. They don't stand a chance!'

'Who doesn't?' Smoke muttered, and with his guns in his hands he dropped on elbows and knees and crawled to the nearest window.

Outside, the kerosene lights were still flaring and they cast their glimmer on to a full two score of men. All of them were without their horses, so evidently the attack had been well planned. Smoke looked intently for the figure of Tarlton but could not spot him in the gloom.

Then more shots exploded, but they were not aimed at the saloon. They had the effect of dousing the lamps so that the street was only starlit.

'You take that window, son, and I'll take this,' Carmichael said, his gross bulk dimly visible nearby. 'Since these mugs want to play games I'm quite willin'.'

'I'm taking this window,' Trixie insisted. 'I've only got a .32 automatic, but it may help.'

'Watch yourself, Trix, for heaven's sake,' Smoke cautioned.

Suddenly Carmichael fired — and that touched off the gunpowder with a vengeance. Realizing there were defenders in the saloon Tarlton and his boys opened up with everything they had got.

A fusillade of shots struck the saloon, shattering the windows and, in some cases, ripping through the wooden walls. Smoke crouched, peering round the edge of the window at intervals and firing quickly. Though he, Trixie, and Carmichael were hopelessly out-numbered they were in a better shooting position than the attackers who had no cover at all. From the dim view of them it was possible to obtain it seemed that some of them were already sprawled on the ground . . .

But the tide of men were coming nearer, some of them taking the chance of diving across the street where, being at too sharp an angle to hit, they were evidently worming their way towards the saloon's closed doors.

Smoke fired three times in quick succession; Trixie fired once. Then shots exploded against the doorway. Carmichael took a chance and leaned through the broken window. He fired three times and his shots were dead on the mark. The two men who had reached the doors dropped with screams of pain, and did not get up again.

Carmichael grinned and began to withdraw, then he gasped with pain as a bullet slashed across the top of his head. He dropped backwards and sagged on the floor, his gun dropping from his hand. Instantly Smoke was at his side.

'Badly hurt?' he asked anxiously, raising Carmichael's head and shoulders.

Carmichael could not speak for a moment or two. Blood was coursing down from his injured head.

'I — I reckon that one got me, but good,' he muttered. 'All I want is the chance t'nail th' critter that did it. I saw him. Give me a hand to get up.'

Smoke did so. Trixie was holding the fort for the moment, her little automatic spitting at intervals. Glass flew out close by her face and she dodged back. Carmichael fought his way back into position, wiping the blood from his forehead, Smoke holding on to him. He took aim and fired and there was a howl of anguish from outside.

Instantly a gun spat back and Smoke felt the fat man start up in pain. Then he fell back heavily, blood dimly visible across his white shirt.

'No — no mistake about that one,' he whispered. 'Guess I'm doin' no more shootin' for yuh, son . . . ' He fought hard for breath. 'Git me a piece of paper, quick — an' a pen.'

Smoke hurtled across to the bar where pen and paper were usually kept. He came back with them to find that Carmichael was nearly out, his head and shoulders supported against Trixie's knee. Outside, all was quiet for the moment. Evidently Tarlton was waiting to see what happened next.

'Gimme a light,' Carmichael whispered. 'Must have a light . . . '

Smoke cupped a lucifer in his hands. In fact he did so three times whilst Carmichael wrote unsteadily on the pad pressed against his upraised knee.

'I reckon that does it,' he murmured at last. 'I know when I'm licked,

Smoke, and this it — I've turned everythin' over to you. Nobody I'd rather let have it. You and Trixie. Pair uv reg'lar shooters — '

The rest of his words were drowned out by a shattering commotion from the doors. They flew back under the onslaught of bullets and man power. Tarlton and his followers came tumbling into the dim saloon.

'Hold it!' Tarlton ordered. 'I c'n just see you, Smoke, and if you fire it's the finish. I'm warning you!'

Smoke remained motionless, waiting to see what happened next. Tarlton gave an order and one of his men lighted the oil lamps. By degrees the glimmering became bright again and Smoke found himself looking at Tarlton and his followers by the doors, their guns aimed. On the floor, at Smoke's feet, Carmichael lay crumpled, Trixie crouched behind him.

Slowly Smoke rose, the last Will of Carmichael balled into his palm. He helped up Trixie and then stood waiting as Tarlton came over.

'Just like I've always said,' Tarlton remarked. 'When you get ditched by so-called laws, the only thing to do is to use a gun. It gets better results than anything — What happened to this fat louse?' he asked, and turned Carmichael over with his boot. When he saw the wounds he gave a hard grin. 'Cashed in his chips at last, huh? Just as well.'

Smoke bent down and picked up the thick scratch pad. He folded it and pushed it in his left hand shirt pocket, then he tossed the screwed up ink bottle to the further corner.

'Guess that finishes everything,' he said, plunging his hands in his pants pockets and thereby getting rid of the paper Carmichael had signed. 'What comes next? Shooting, I suppose?'

'Naturally.' Tarlton gave a grim smile. 'Neat trick of mine, huh, to call off everybody so's you couldn't get any help?'

'They'll come back thirsting for your

blood, Tarlton, and you know it!'

'Yeah? I've got an answer to that too. I'm going to have every homestead in the district ransacked and, in places, burned down. And I'll blame it all on to you. When the folks come back I'll tell 'em the gold strike was a trick of yours, not mine, so's you could rob everywhere. You're only a saddle-tramp at heart, remember, and might easily think up a neat dodge to do a spot of robbery and then vamoose. That's the story I'm goin' to tell and my boys here will back me up. I'll tell 'em I took charge when you'd been hounded out of the district — and the mugs'll believe me because they'll have to.'

'Got it all sewn up, haven't you?' Smoke asked bitterly.

'Yeah. Well planned. As for you, you're taking a ride — a corpse on a horse, and I aim to start right now . . . '

Tarlton's gun cocked and the hammer drew back.

'As for Trixie,' he finished, 'I'm keeping her around. I guess she's too nice to rub out and in spite of everything she's done to me I've always figgered on marrying her. An' I shall. Certainly she won't talk about what's happened, 'less she wants a taste of what she got last time.'

Abruptly, knowing it was the finish if he didn't move, Smoke flung himself forward. But he was not quick enough. Tarlton's gun exploded and a smoking hole drilled itself directly on Smoke's heart. He caught at himself desperately, gasped, and then pitched helplessly on his face. Instantly Trixie dived for him, but the men around her dragged her back.

'Take him out,' Tarlton snapped. 'Tie him to a horse and drive it as far as the desert. Fasten it up there and let it rot with his corpse on it. Mebbe a lesson to any other mugs who think they can poke their noses in.'

Smoke's limp form was hoisted between four of the men and carried out of the saloon. Trixie watched dumbly and then turned back to Tarlton. He was grinning at her sadistically.

'Right back where we started, eh Trix?' he asked. 'You don't have to worry, kid, I'm not going to manhandle you — not if you keep your mouth shut and do as you're told . . . I guess we all wait here — all night if need be — until those mugs on the phony gold strike come running back. The moment they do I've a story to tell, and you fellas see you bear it out. Otherwise you'll eat lead. Same goes for you, Trix.'

The girl did not answer. She moved to the nearest chair and sank into it, burying her blonde head in her hands. For her, the world had ended.

In a detached fashion she was aware of the men moving about the saloon, getting drinks for themselves. Then she realised that Carmichael's heavy body had disappeared — evidently taken outside and buried with the usual lack of ceremony in which Tarlton delighted.

It seemed to her that many hours passed while she sat in the chair, cold and cramped, Tarlton not very far from her, his venomous eyes hardly once leaving her. The tension was only broken when at last there came the sound of feet tramping in the main street and the murmur of voices. Before very long men and women began to come through the batwings, pausing as they beheld Tarlton and his henchmen and the weary, dejected girl.

'Well, my lucky gold prospectors, what now?' Tarlton asked drily.

'What in hell are you doing here, Tarlton?' one of the men demanded. 'Where's the sheriff? Who's responsible for some of our ranches and home-steads burning? We saw 'em as we came back into town.'

'The sheriff was responsible.' Tarlton got on his feet, and then he reeled off the story he had already outlined to Smoke. The men and women listened in silence, their faces grim.

'I reckon that's hard to believe,' one of the men said. 'I'd kinda gotten it fixed in my head that Smoke was a regular guy.'

'He meant you to,' Tarlton responded, shrugging. 'But don't forget he came from no place and became sheriff at his own suggestion. He blew dust in the eyes of the lot of you, only waiting for the time when he could get all of you out of the way, steal everything he could find, and then vamoose.'

'And yuh say yuh took care of him?' a woman demanded. 'Where is he now, anyways?'

'Dead! I shot him myself, right through the heart. Then I had my boys take him out into the desert. He can rot there. The kind of game he pulled he ain't worthy of a grave.'

'Guess Tarlton's telling the truth,' one of the gunmen remarked. 'We saw the thing happen.'

'Yeah?' asked a cattleman. 'All seems mighty convenient to me. Too convenient! What happened to the stuff Smoke was supposed to have stolen?'

'What d'you mean, supposed?' Tarlton barked. 'If you're doubting my word — '

'The stuff's all buried just outside the town,' another gunman said — the one who had organized the homestead robbing during the past two hours. 'You'll find it there. Smoke confessed to it before the boss plugged him.'

A man in the forefront of the returned crowd spat in the sawdust.

'I don't believe a word of it!' he declared flatly. 'We never caught Smoke out on a dirty deal but we did catch you! That wheel, fur one thing — '

'Lies, lies, lies!' Trixie screamed suddenly, leaping up. 'I can't sit here any longer and listen to Mark telling you such stories — He killed Smoke. Shot him like he said — but Smoke didn't do anything. He organized that phony gold strike! Him! Mark Tarl — '

She went flying backwards from the impact of Tarlton's hand. Catching at a chair she saved herself from falling. Tarlton, who had had his hands on his guns, suddenly yanked them out — and so did his men around him.

'All right, so I misjudged,' he said, his

voice hard. 'I figgered I could make you believe me, but evidently you're smarter than I thought . . . '

Nobody spoke. The men and women kept their hands up.

'I've about forty men here all loyal to me,' Tarlton continued. 'And from here on I'm taking over where I left off. We'll run the town at the point of a gun if we have to — but we'll run it! And you mugs will do just as I say. Lefty, take their hardware from them. That's a good start to making 'em see sense.'

It took Lefty a good ten minutes to collect the firearms then at Tarlton's instructions he dumped them behind the bar.

'Yuh can't get away with this, Tarlton,' one of the cattlemen said.

'Who can't? I'm doing nicely so far.'

'So far, yes — but how do you think yuh can keep all of us nailed down once we leave here? Just can't be done. An' there are more uv us than there are uv your men.'

'If any of you attempt anything,'

Tarlton said slowly, 'I will kill three of you in return. Preferably wipe out a whole family at once. You, McElroy, for instance you've got a wife, son and daughter. If you tried to kill one of my men, and succeeded, I'd have you, your wife, and kids all hanged in your own orchard. Think that over, the lot of you, because I mean it.'

'Yore loco, man,' a puncher growled. 'A gun-happy coyote on a blood hunt, an' nothing else.'

Tarlton mentioned his guns. 'I'm ignoring that right now, Clancy, but I'll pay you back for it later. You can all get out — and quick. And don't forget what I told you.'

He turned and seized Trixie's arm, whirling her to her feet.

'As for you, Trix, I didn't like the way you shot your mouth off just now. Mebbe you're in need of another lesson — '

'You mean you are!' a voice snapped from the batwings, and simultaneously a shot exploded. It blew Tarlton's gun out of his right hand and set blood brimming into his palm.

Astounded and pain-twisted he gazed at the figure of Smoke pushing through the crowd. Immediately the guns of Tarlton's men came up, but Tarlton stopped them.

'Hold it, fellers. If you fire at him he'll get me first. I'm not taking that risk — '

'Smoke!' Trixie nearly screamed, hurtling over to him. 'I — I thought you were dead! I — I saw Mark here shoot you right in the heart.'

Smoke did not answer her. He gave her arm an encouraging grip and then moved nearer to Tarlton, still covering him with the gun.

'You got the idea right, Tarlton,' he said deliberately. 'If your men fire at me I'll get you before I drop — '

Tarlton could only stare, still completely dazed. His eyes wandered to the bullet hole in Smoke's shirt, just over his heart.

'We can settle this in our own way,'

Smoke added. 'Have your men throw their hardware away for the moment. You've cleaned out the guns of these townsfolk here, so that makes it equal. When that's done I'll throw my gun aside too.'

'What d'you suppose I can do with my hand blasted?' Tarlton demanded 'Fight?'

'You've one hand good. I'll only use one, too. That makes it equal. Better do it, Tarlton. I've the drop on you.'

Tarlton jerked his head and with sullen faces his men obeyed, tossing their guns over to the bar counter. They came back empty handed, wondering. Smoke gave a quick glance about him and then put his own gun back in its holster. He unfastened his belt and tossed it away along the floor.

'What the heck's the idea of this?' Tarlton demanded, screwing his kerchief round his wounded hand. 'You trying to settle an issue, or what?'

'Yeah — an outstanding one. Nothing to do with this saloon. This place is mine now Carmichael's dead, and right here in my pocket I've got a Will of his which says so. Any authorities will uphold that. It's another matter I'm sorting out with you, Tarlton — and you're going to talk!'

On the last word Smoke lashed out his right hand, seized Tarlton about his sound wrist, and then twisted with all his strength. Gasping, helpless in the steel clutch, Tarlton twirled round and dropped on his knees. His arm was forced up his back with crushing pressure. This, coupled with the fact that his other hand was useless, made him helpless.

'Now, I've got an arm-lock on you, Tarlton, which will dislocate your shoulder if I want it that way. The one chance you've got of stopping me, is by making a confession, before everybody.'

'Confession?' Tarlton turned a drawn, sweating face for a moment. 'Confession about what?'

'That murder you committed in Denver, and fixed it so Trixie looked like the culprit . . . '

Trixie gave a start and the men and women looked at each other in surprise. Tarlton made a savage effort to tear free, but instead his arm went further up his back. It went higher still and he could feel the bone grinding murderously in his shoulder socket.

'I know all about it,' Smoke added grimly. 'Better admit the truth — or else.'

Tarlton writhed and twisted helplessly, but he could not dislodge the grip. He began to draw sharp breaths as the pain of his slowly dislocating shoulder tore at him. This, coupled with the anguish of his wounded hand, was getting more than he could bear.

'All right — I fixed it,' he panted. 'I — I shot the guy. Sudden murderous temper came over me, I guess. I dunno how I got that way. I fixed it so as to make Trix think she was guilty so's I'd have an excuse for keeping her right beside me — '

'That's all I need to know, Cavendish,'

a quiet voice said.

Smoke released his hold and Tarlton slowly straightened up. Through the haze of his pain and confusion he realized that a powerfully built marshal was eyeing him, his gun cocked.

'It's a fix,' Tarlton gasped hoarsely. 'Smoke, you double-crossed me!'

'I made you talk, to save time,' Smoke replied. 'This is Captain Bannister, a law officer. But for him I might have died out in the desert — not from that bullet you fired at me, but from thirst, and the fact that I couldn't get free of that horse I was tied to. 'Captain Bannister came along just in time and spotted me in the moonlight. He was on his way to Hell's Acres anyways, looking for you, Tarlton. When that other law officer didn't report, Bannister here came to investigate. It was you that other man was looking for, Tarlton — not Trixie. They'd found her bullet — which had missed — embedded in the wall. But it didn't match that found in the body! They'd worked things out, but the one thing they needed was a confession, so I told Bannister I'd get it, before witnesses. I did.'

Tarlton breathed hard, but there was nothing he could do. Bannister motioned with his gun.

'Better get your weapons back, you people,' he said, with a glance at the townsfolk. 'You'll want to try these followers of Tarlton in your own way later on. As for you, Tarlton, you can have your hand dressed, then you're coming with me. The charges against you are murder — for the Denver City business and the death of Clayburn, the blacksmith.'

Tarlton had nothing left to say. In silence, holding his wounded hand, he watched Smoke put an arm round Trixie's shoulders.

'It's a miracle,' she whispered. 'You being alive, Smoke.'

He grinned and pulled a folded notepad out of his shirt pocket. The thick papers were nearly drilled through with a bullet.

'No miracle, Trix,' he said, tossing the pad on the floor. 'The pad stopped the bullet, but the blow over the heart keeled me out for the moment. I guess you played your last trick there, Tarlton, and lost it.'

THE END

We do hope that you have enjoyed reading this large print book.

Did you know that all of our titles are available for purchase?

We publish a wide range of high quality large print books including:
Romances, Mysteries, Classics
General Fiction
Non Fiction and Westerns

Special interest titles available in large print are:
The Little Oxford Dictionary
Music Book, Song Book
Hymn Book, Service Book

Also available from us courtesy of Oxford University Press:
Young Readers' Dictionary
(large print edition)
Young Readers' Thesaurus
(large print edition)

For further information or a free brochure, please contact us at:
Ulverscroft Large Print Books Ltd.,
The Green, Bradgate Road, Anstey,
Leicester, LE7 7FU, England.
Tel: (00 44) **0116 236 4325**
Fax: (00 44) **0116 234 0205**

Farmer Will Pickle's life was a peaceful one until the day his wife died and he lost his farm. Bank president Mike Herman thought it a good joke to make Will the sheriff. But things didn't go as Herman had planned. And Will, now up against plenty of enemies, found his greatest challenge was Crazy Charles. Life in lawless times forced Will to live by the rule, kill or be killed — and he was more than able to oblige.

SMOKY HILL TRAIL

Mark Falcon

When the Denver Bank threatened to repossess his family home and land, eighteen-year-old Jed Stone unwillingly became involved in a robbery with his neighbours, the four McIver brothers. The McIvers got away with the strongbox, but Jed was sentenced, under an assumed name, to five years in the Kansas Penitentiary. On his release, two women came into his life as he returned home to get his share of the hold-up money. That was when the trouble would really begin!

AYLI VALLEY

Gary Astill

Owen Lismore has to leave the lovely Rosalind behind when he goes on the run from his brother and the notorious gunman Josh Bassinet. But when Owen's best friend is killed by Bassinet, he knows he can never rest easy while the gunman lives. Despite all the dire warnings about his chances against the killer, Owen rides in for the showdown . . .